KING

Love is not always clean

The Broken Bows *Kerri Ann*
Book 1

BY

KERRI ANN

Kerri Ann
Contemporary Romance Author

Mother of two insanely (well trained) sarcastic men, wife to a dangerously smolder inducing grumble bunny (fireman), and friend to some amazing ladies (you know who you are). Thanks for reading, thanks for being a friend, and I look forward to meeting you in the future for drinks, danger and laughs.

Living in Northern Ontario, Canada, Kerri loves to read, travel and find new reasons to write you fantastic love stories. Remember, not all love is clean. Dark, light, angsty, sexually charged and twisted—that's her genre.

It's heart wrenching stories where the muse directs her. As the instrument of their lives, their stories are told through piece by piece. You can hope for the good guy to win, but it won't always happen. She can't guarantee an HEA (happily ever after) or HFN (happy for now), because life doesn't always have those.

Enjoy the OMG's and tears. Tear your hair out, toss a book or two, because I want you to feel their pain too. As they live it, you can absorb it on the pages.

Website: www.authorkerriann.com

BookBub: www.bookbub.com/authors/kerri-ann

Instagram: www.instagram.com/authorkerriann

Facebook page: www.facebook.com/LoveandDreams

Twitter: www.twitter.com/Daresanddreams

Join my newsletter to hear what's coming soon, view spoilers that others haven't seen yet, and keep up to date on my insanity.

Newsletter goo.gl/YAJFbr

Don't want the antics and fun to stop? Become one of Kerri Ann's Dirty Little Heart Breakers.

www.facebook.com/groups/1218799488152517/

TABLE OF CONTENTS

Dedicated to those that are lost and need to be found again…

To know your future,
you need the past…
To fix the future,
you have to own *now*.

CHAPTER 1

Busta

Sitting in the bar, I'm enjoying my fifth Jim Beam as I wait for church. Others are enjoying their old ladies or the hang arounds, playing pool, or just having a toke or two as they drink and fuck around. A normal afternoon in the Broken Bows San Bernardino Chapter. We're on lockdown after one of our shipments was hit earlier last week. The space is pretty full and the tension is high.

With clanging, screams, and the sound of breaking dishes coming from the kitchen area, Panna, one of the old ladies, walks out with her hands in the air. "I'm out of this one, Busta. This is someone else's problem."

The clamoring continues as the ladies spill out, each with their hands up in defeat, walking directly to the dark recesses of the clubhouse.

"Pan?"

Shaking her head and rolling her eyes, the wrinkles on her face crease further. "That fucking menace has got to go. She's tearing down the kitchen, all because Gazie doesn't know how to make a cream sauce." Retribution's old lady is a clear-headed woman. I've learned to trust her judgement over the years on most things, and she's a beauty too. At almost forty-nine, you'd swear she was thirty-five. Jet-black hair, not a stray gray to be seen, bright eyes that see everything, and a complexion that's clearer of wrinkles than the whores that hang around. She's one sexy ol' lady.

As the crashing sounds continue from the kitchen, I rise off the chair. "Thanks, Pan." Kissing her forehead and walking toward the door, she smiles at me before searching out Ret. Turning to two of the guys, I start for the door. "Miss, Nock—with me."

By the sounds of it, we'll need more than one of us for this shit.

Pulling the door back and stepping inside, I nearly lose my head from a plate that soars across the room.

"Who the fuck threw that!" I yell, my dark voice booming across the space. Backing up slightly, I nearly knock Miss on his ass.

"What the fuck was that!" he crows out on a laugh.

"Stupid fucking cunts," Nock growls. And I can't disagree.

As I try again to enter, I hear Scarlet's panicked voice. "Busta! Over here! Help!" I can't see her, but it sounds urgent. She's another level-headed woman. Not my favorite by any means, but it takes a lot to set her off.

With another plate soaring past, I yell out, "Jesus fucking Christ! Whoever's throwing shit, I won't think twice about knocking you out if I get hit. Fucking hold your shit up." Turning around in the space, I don't see anyone. Not a fucking surprise, though. Our kitchen is an L-shaped room, with the cupboards veering off to the left, and the oversized subzero fridge blocking the view around the corner.

"Nock, figure that shit out. Scarlet, where the fuck are you?"

"Over here! Hurry!" With a hand sticking up in the air from behind the island, I walk toward her, watching for projectiles as I move. True's old lady, Scarlet, is a tough bitch, so if she's hiding, there has to be a good reason.

Making my way around the island, I find Scarlet holding a dish towel against Gazelle. Laid out on the floor, a knife buried deep in her shoulder, the pale little waif is unconscious and flat out on her back.

I search for a pulse. "Fuck me. What the hell happened, Scarlet?"

With her chin raised toward the corner by the subzero, she glares hard. "That fucking lunatic lost it over some stupid shit. Mona was cutting chicken breasts on the far side of the room, bitching that Gazelle was a useless virgin cunt that didn't deserve to be anywhere near a man like Munch. Gazie shot back at her with a smart remark about being a virgin but not dumb like Mona, and that's when all hell broke loose. Busta, I was standing by Gazie. She just missed me and Pan."

Her hands are coated in blood, and even as we hide out, worrying about how to get Gazie out of here, dishes are still crashing around the room.

"Nock, get that shit locked down!" I yell.

"Fuck, man! I'm on it, I'm on it. She just lobbed a pan at Miss. He's down now too."

Growling her disproval, Scarlet captures my attention with a blood-soaked hand. "She's gotta get to the hospital, Busta."

"Yeah. Keep pressure there."

Rising, just as a pot flies by, I curse. "Fuck, Mona! Quit your shit!"

I hope to fuck she runs out of ammo soon. Turning, I find Miss laid out cold with a goose egg on his forehead.

When I rush over and stand behind the door, Nock laughs. "We won't have a fucking meal if she keeps this up." He's always a silly fucker. Always finding the lighter side to anything. Thing is, I know how much he loves food, so if he's making light of it, he's got a plan.

With another pan slamming against the door, I yell back over the clanging, "She destroys the kitchen and we won't be eatin' anything but fucking takeout pizzas for a week."

"Yeah, but if we rush her, there's a good chance knives will fly." Motioning for me to follow him toward the door, he smirks. "I've got an idea."

Popping back out to the common room, narrowly missing a knife sticking in the top of the door, he laughs again. It's a nervous thing with him. He thinks everything's funny, especially when it's some fucked up shit. "I'm gonna grab Munch. No one but him can settle that twisted tit," he says, heading toward the bunkie. I follow him, thinking he's on the right path.

The bunkie is just off the main house. It's a large stone, two-story that houses close to twenty guys and their old ladies. I don't stay here much, as I have my own place, but it's always full, and that means it's always busy around the club. I like my solitude and privacy. I have my reasons for it, and for the most part, they leave me be.

The club compound is a total of three buildings, one being the Pres's residence. There's the low, one-story converted machine shop that houses the clubhouse and garage, and the cement block that houses the guys. We didn't have enough space in the main building after the garage and church were situated.

Munch has been hiding out, avoiding Gazelle for days, so I doubt he has any idea this is going on. Nock is right. If anyone can diffuse this, it's Munch.

Stepping in, the air conditioning blasts us immediately. Some fucker has turned it down again. When I find out who, his ass will pay the bill. Since DG's death sentence, thanks to cancer, there's been a few that think they can do as they please. As Enforcer, it's been my responsibility to keep the bills low so we can help with his drugs.

He has lung cancer, stage four. He wouldn't opt for a hospital, and he couldn't bring himself to go through chemo or radiation either. He knew it would hold him back from riding. DG would rather cough up a lung through a trip than not be able to ride at all.

Over the years, he's worked toward his twins, True and Strike, into taking over the positions of Pres and VP. The two of them are identical in every way—except for their idea of the club. Only Bracken, better known as True, is ready to take the gavel. Strike, or Kyden, left before I'd been patched in five years earlier. I've only ever seen him at community functions a handful of times, and the first time I mistook him for True. It was a Halloween event, and I thought he was fucking around, dressing as a priest. I wouldn't make that mistake again after he tried to bless me for my sins.

Making our way down to Munch's door, I knock hard. "Open up, Munch!"

"Fuck off, Busta. I'm not in the mood," he snaps.

"Mona knifed Gazie," Nock states matter-of-factly, before grinning at me.

That'll get his ass up.

Before I have a chance to pound the door again, Munch pulls it open. "What the fuck are you talkin' about?"

"Mona lost her shit and threw a butcher knife at Gazie. We called an ambo for her—"

As he pushes past us both and races down the hall to the light of day, Nock jokes, "Well that worked."

"Maybe next time, we don't lead with that."

"It worked, didn't it?"

Shaking my head at him and closing Munch's door, Nock and I make our way back to the common room. Stepping inside, the only thing I hear is him losing his shit.

"That's e-fucking-nuff, woman!"

On the best of days, Munch is an extreme guy. I've gone toe-to-toe with him a few times in the gym and even I don't compare to him. I'm not a slouch by any means, but I can't bench three times my weight. That, and he throws a mean left hook. He's surprised me more than once with that little rocker, cleaning my clock and making my teeth rattle.

Colton, better known as Munch for his affection to eat pussy, is like Strike, True, and myself—we're lifers. Born into club life, guided by our parents. They wanted him to be the Sargent at Arms—sure as fuck had the size and scary shit down pat—but his mind wasn't in it. He's better suited to Treasurer. The man's got a thing for numbers. He's helped to further the club's holdings by legal means in the last three years. Of course, not all things are legal, but he's increased my stocks tenfold in pot sales this year alone.

Noticing the stillness of the area, and not hearing any more plates or pots crashing, my hopes are that he slowed her down. Waiting across the room, the two ambo attendants are wide-eyed as they take in the room full of hard-ass bikers. Beside them are Nock and Miss, who's being checked over for a concussion.

"What the fuck's goin' on in here!" The distinct yell reverberates off the walls. Crossing the room from the direction of church, DG stands there, red in the face, surly and pissed off. Even as he looks sullen and diseased, he's still a threatening man. This year, he's lost at least forty pounds, and while it was necessary, he looks sickly compared to the strong man we've come to know.

Moving to stand by me, where I'm leaning on the wall with my arms crossed, he raises his chin, asking for an explanation. "Mona was re-decorating the kitchen. A few have taken damage." I motion to Miss, who's still a bit cloudy, with a whiskey in hand and a whore's hand down his jeans. It's obvious he'll recover quickly.

"So what the fuck are they here for? We don't normally need ambos for that shit." He means Taught, the resident doc.

Pursing my lips, I shake my head. "Won't help her," I inform him, as Gazie's being wheeled out the door, an attendant crouched over her working chest compressions.

As Munch steps out of the kitchen, dragging his bastard daughter by her hair, he snaps, "Someone do something with this bitch. I can't." Tossing her to the nearest brother, she struggles. As Munch moves to follow the attendants out, holding Gazelle's hand lovingly, I see the struggle in his eyes. This is killing him. His daughter and the girl he's crazy about are at war. I can't imagine that. Pussy whipped motherfucker.

I pray to all the fucking bike gods—Harley, Honda, Norton, and Triumph—that I don't find an old lady in the future. I'm more than glad to be the single cocky bastard I am. If I found a woman that suited me, it'd be a fucking miracle. No one so far has gone toe-to-toe with me. She hasn't even been invented as far as I'm concerned.

Turning to Smart, the man holding the psycho cunt now, I inform him on what to do. "Lock her in a room—a special one. We'll deal with her after church." Not me, but someone will. We'll escort her off club property when the time's right, and she won't be back. You don't attack another member, patched or not.

As the ambo screeches out of the compound, lights and sirens wailing, Munch walks back in. His hands are covered in blood, and his usual smirk is replaced with a dark and sullen stare. It alerts all in his vicinity not to speak ill of sweet Gazelle right now. He'd cut a brother without thought.

"Are you all ready to get to work?" DG states harshly as he shuffles across the room. "Church. Now."

Leaving no room for argument, we all follow obediently.

Catching up to Munch, who's slamming his phone and keys in the tray outside the door, I say, "She'll be fine. Girl is gritty."

With a simple head nod, he bypasses me to his seat.

CHAPTER 2

Busta

Coughing into a rag, we wait for DG to gather his composure. As the weeks have passed, DG has deteriorated before our eyes. True has taken over more and more of the president's responsibilities by giving directives, lifting a finger at the heavy stuff, and becoming the man his father wanted him to be. He's made decisions I never thought DG would never allow—not even one of his sons.

He's always been more dictator than president. It's the first thing you learn about him before being patched in. Personally, I've always been fine with it, as he's never led us astray, and I have bigger worries than if someone wants to tell me what to do.

Not one to mince words, as the last brother walks through the door, DG starts in. "What's the verdict on Diesel?"

Diesel's father, Victory, perks up immediately, knowing the request was directed at him. "He's out of surgery. They were able to graft most of the road rash on his leg, but his hand is done. He won't ride again."

Fuck. Not what we'd all hoped to hear. Diesel, Nock, Victory, and I were on a run last week when we were ambushed by a rival club. Diesel was at the back, watching for issues with our transport van. Nock was driving the van when someone blew out his rear tire, causing Diesel to go over his handlebars at eighty miles an hour. We lost the shipment.

This has gotta be wrecking him. It nearly wrecked me when I was trying to keep him calm as we waited for the ambulance to arrive. The skin peeled away to the bone on his leg, and both his hands were mangled, as he'd tried to save himself from the fall. I know he'll be lucky to pick up a fork, never mind turn a throttle.

Fuckin' bullshit.

I know if someone told me I wouldn't ride again, I'd just eat a bullet and call it quits. I've been on a bike for as long as I can remember.

Pulling me back to the task at hand, DG coughs harshly for a moment. More and more, his body is talking, but he's not listening. He needs to slow down. Finally getting a few gulps of air, he asks, "Where are we on the fucking cocksuckers that rolled Diesel and the shipment? I went on your intel, Miss. I thought we had the support of The Four Horsemen in their territory?"

That meant we'd give them a cut of what we ran through their territory, and they'd keep out of our business. Miss had worked it all out with their Sargent at Arms, Destroyer, and after I left the hospital, I'd called him straightaway. Miss was fucking livid. Can't say I trust anyone implicitly, but their man Destroyer was as surprised as I was that we'd been hit after the dealings we'd set up. "Pres, I had an understanding with the SA. If the Restless Souls were able to get the jump on us on Horsemen's turf, then something fuckin' fishy's going on."

I interject, turning DG's ire and fire my way, and away from Miss and his slightly sore head. "I've got a meet with Death tomorrow. If his club's behind this, I'll put the bullet in his head myself."

Happy with the answer, DG nods and continues. "Fine. Make sure that fucker knows who he's dealin' with. Don't roll over and show your belly."

I grind my teeth. "Not about to." I'm pissed he thinks I'd be a pushover. The last thing I do is show my belly to anyone. But I'm not about to start a fight with DG in church, so I hold in my remark and bite my tongue.

"Good. Now, who wants to tell me what that shit was with the whores?"

Looking to Munch, I see his jaw set to correct whoever'd call Gazie a whore, but being that it's DG, he composes himself quickly. "Mona's in lockdown. We'll deal with her. Gazelle had a pretty nasty injury. By the sounds of it, she'll need surgery. I'll head to the hospital to check on her after church."

Shaking his head, DG slams a hand down on the table. "No you fuckin' won't! The whores aren't important. Get your head in the game, Munch. We need everyone to put their full effort into the Horsemen and Restless Souls. This club has always been the strength, so for someone to get the drop on us, we're weak somewhere." When he coughs this time, blood stains his cloth. "Balls to the wall, boys." He slams a pistol down on the table. "You're either in this, or I'll put a bullet between your eyes now. I don't have an issue with putting a cunt out of his misery."

Shit. Guns are dropped at the door to church. DG may run this club, but to threaten us in church is a dark move. He's losing it.

"Have you lost your mind? It's fuckin' church, Dad," True snaps, voicing what we're all thinking. As True reaches for the pistol, DG lifts it, pointing it directly at his son's forehead.

"Try me, boy." The air is thick, palpable and deadly, and then he clicks the safety off. "You'll be the first to go. I don't care if you're blood. Strike and you shoulda been lookin' after this club. I should be relaxing." Resting the barrel on True, DG looks ready to kill. "I swear this club has gone weak because of cunts like you." He then looks around the room at all of us, pointing the gun at me, Munch, then Flight. "Diesel wouldn't be in a hospital. All you cunts are to blame! I don't trust a fuckin' one of ya anymore."

Fuck. This is escalating fast. I don't dare tear my eyes away from DG for fear of what he's capable of, but in the back of the room, I can hear the distinct click of a gun's safety coming off. Raising a hand, motioning for whoever it is at the back to calm their shit, I stand up slowly.

Staring down DG, I show him I'm not afraid. "Go ahead, I fucking dare you. Don't disrespect my resolve to this club, DG. I've supported you, giving you my all. There isn't a day that I've thought of anything other than the good of this club. So if you're gonna shoot me, you fucking better make it count."

His eyes are trained on me—menacing, dark, and without remorse. DG has no issues with showing his dominance—never has—but this is outside the usual cock posturing.

Like staring down a bull, waiting to see who'll break first, Devil's Guide and I square off. Crossing my arms and narrowing my gaze, I wait him out. As time ticks down, I hear the nervous breathing of everyone in the room. They're seeing the breakdown of something so important. Church is cleared of weapons because it's a room of openness and conversation; a space that's free of threats. This is wrong.

This moment will have repercussions.

Clicking the safety back on, allowing the gun to hang from his index finger, DG offers it to True before moving from his seat. "The women have more balls than you. Get your shit together. Church's over."

Walking out, I understand that DG has adjusted the dynamics.

Fuck.

CHAPTER 3

Busta

"Busta!" I hear as I'm walking out of church. Turning, there stands True. Slapping me on the shoulder, his look is dark—darker than usual. Guiding us down the hall, he directs us to his quarters. "Sorry about Dad. It's getting outta hand. We need to find a resolution to this."

I don't disagree. DG is becoming volatile. Church today is another example of how his control is waning. He's failing in health and his strength is dwindling—so what does he do? He attacks us. The loyal bastards that would never cause the club harm. True has had a few conversations with me in private about what to do about his dad. I know about his plan to take over soon, and so far, I've avoided all conversations about it. But it seems I can't avoid it any longer.

Shutting the door, he locks it and steps over to his minibar. Pulling out two beers, he offers me one. "I have a job for you."

I pop the top. "I guess this isn't a church thing."

True takes a large gulp of his drink. "I see the failures going on. I know what the other clubs think. *We* need to finish this, and soon."

Crossing my arms, I lean against the wall, waiting for True to deliver his request. "You're heading to meet with Death, yeah?"

I nod and take a sip of beer.

"I need you to suss out the Four Horsemen. Don't fail me. Don't fail the club. Got me?" He holds out his hand. His expectation is that I'm on his side—that I'm against DG, our president, and the leader of the Broken Bows.

Gulping down my brew, I consider my answer carefully. One wrong word, and True could put me in a position that can cause me issues. It's a hard line to ride. "Yeah. I got ya."

"Good. There's only a few I trust now." He leans back in his chair. "You, Nock, and Miss are it. I'll be adjusting things when Dad's gone, and you my friend will see an advancement." Kicking his feet up on the table, he gives me that sinister sneer he's perfected. "Trust is a big thing. I need to surround myself with boys I trust."

Trust. Sometimes I forget they don't understand my sacrifices. They don't know my past, and I'm keeping it that way. If I have any power in my future, they'll never know. My past will never creep into the present.

But that's the thing with the past: it always comes back to bite you in the ass when you least expect it.

"Get a feel for Death. Last thing we need is the Horsemen going sideways on us."

Sucking back the rest of my beer, I set it on the table by his feet before opening the door to the hall, but I turn and say, "I'll let you know soon."

CHAPTER 4

Busta

I'm led to the back of the Humble Club, a gentleman's club in Anaheim. I've only met Curse a handful of times, and from what I've seen, he's a fair enough guy. I've heard the president is the same kind of man, and decent.

Once at the back, I find Death sitting there, smug and in charge. "You must be Busta. What do ya say we get down to the business at hand." He holds out a hand for me to shake, showing dominance over the situation. "You know my VP, Curse."

I keep my eyes on Death, knowing he's giving my Broken Bows cut a once-over. Normally, you don't wear your colors into a bar, or into the bar of another club, but this is a special meet up where we're seeing whose dick is bigger.

Mine. No contest.

I remain standing, giving a chin lift to Curse. Both men are tall and broad. Clearly, they hit the gym on the regular, and they're both scarred. Curse has crinkled skin on the right side of his face, tight and pulled, obviously from a fire of some sort. I've never asked. Giving him a strong and solid look, he could assume I'm staring, but I don't give a shit. It is as it is. Death, though, is a man I've looked into.

I made inquiries, wanting to be sure I was well-versed in the Four Horsemen before I came for the meet. As a second-generation president, he's a respected leader, which is more than I can say recently for the Bows. Death is strong-willed, dependable, loyal, and will kill on sight if one of his is threatened. I respect that. His father, Mayhem, died two years back of a heart attack while riding, crashing into the side of a semi. It left Death with his sister, Jasmine, and a little brother, Jason, who hasn't been patched in yet, but is working on it I hear.

I'm of a mixed heritage, but Death's native complexion makes him darker than me. His light brown eyes are searching mine for something, and that grin of his hints to mischief. There's an old knife scar on his neck, and his cheek has a gouge that was stitched up improperly. There's also a chunk missing from his right earlobe. "Want a drink, Busta?"

"Yeah." I take a seat. "A whiskey would be fine."

He motions for a waitress. "Crystal, two whiskeys, and one of whatever Oubliette wants to create. Tell her to make it sour."

Looking up, I find none other than Crystal, True's half-sister. She recognizes me and flinches. Spinning on her high heels, moving to leave, she upends her tray to the floor. Rocking back on her high pegs, she squats to pick up the mess.

"Fucking menace," Curse mutters loudly.

"It's good. Just grab another tray, Crystal. Clean that up later." Death taps Curse on the shoulder, smiling, watching her bend in the near cunt-exposing outfit.

She rises up with a fearful smile. "Death, I'm—"

"It's cool. Grab our drinks. We have things to talk about."

Walking away, she hangs her head in defeat. I don't have time to worry about why she's here, what her problem is, or if her family knows she's here. It doesn't matter. This meet does.

"Sorry 'bout her." He smirks, watching her walk off. "She has her uses." Clapping his hands together, he leans back. "How 'bout you tell me the reason for this meetup? What's going on with the Bows?"

Fine. Straight to it.

"You gettin' into the skin trade?" I ask.

Pursing his lips, worrying the inside of his cheek, Death nods his head back and forth.

"We might've found an avenue. Someone you pissed off came asking for our help in their supply chain."

"Alta Noche, I assume?"

"Mario's boss didn't like his last few shipments and asked for our input. We already offer him a very lucrative dry goods supply, and this was a wise choice for them." Death is smug, thinking it's a win-win for the Horsemen. He doesn't get we gave up our business with Mario on purpose. Mario was killing off product that didn't suit his clients and dropping them back in Bows' territory for the authorities to find. It was causing heat and harming our well-paying customers. He can keep Mario's division without argument. True and DG deal with the leader directly, and Mario's bullshit is off the books mostly. It's dangerous.

"So you're keeping a client satisfied, that's what I'm gathering. Not looking to branch out in your supply chain."

Before he can answer, a sweet and lyrical voice asks, "Someone asked for a Puckered Asshole?" Venturing my gaze upward, I take in the woman that arrives with a tray laden with drinks. She has a bright smile, blemish free face, long, golden blonde hair, neatly set back from her perfect, make-up free features. Wearing dangly earrings, a tight tank, and skin-tight jeans that show off her thin waist and thick hips, she's fucking gorgeous.

"What the fuck did you make me, Oubliette?"

She grins wide. "You asked for something sour. Enjoy." Setting his drink on the table before him, she places mine and Curse's down within reach.

Taking in my cut, she smirks before walking off.

Quirky.

Gathering up my whiskey, the other two do the same. Right now, I don't have time to think about her, even though I like the looks of her. I have a job to do.

"How about you and I come to an understanding? We won't fight you on Alta Noche. If you feel like stepping out and broadening your horizons, you give us a shout first." Lifting my drink for a tap, I wait for their reply.

After exchanging looks in a silent conversation, Death and Curse come to an agreement. "If your wildcard VP decides to change the rules, though, all bets are off."

Can't say I can control that loose cannon, but I'll do my best. "Agreed." Clinking our glasses, each of us drink to the truce on the

skin trade in San Bernardino and the Anaheim
area.

CHAPTER 5

Oubliette

"Crystal!" Sliding to the far end of the bar, dragging her attention back to her job, Crystal, our newest server, jumps at my mention of her name. She's a fucking wreck. "Clear the other end," I tell her, thoroughly exasperated at her lack of skill.

Yesterday, she dropped a whole tray of highballs filled with over two hundred dollars' worth of whiskey. She would've been fired on the spot, but the client paid for it as she cried. He also bought the rest of the bottle and offered to buy a whole new set of glasses for the bar.

The truth of it is, is that Crystal should be a stripper, not a server. The guys love her assets. But I think she's too sweet to be one of the strippers in the club. She's young, innocent, and pliable. They'd destroy her.

The recently turned twenty-one-year-old— at least that's what her driver's license says— can twist like a bendy straw. I have a running bet with Jazzy on how many of the members have now tried her out. I'm thinking at least ten. Jazzy argued. She thinks it's closer to twenty. Thing is, Crystal's only worked here for three weeks. She's a menace. She set fire to the dancer's change room. She caught a heel in the VIP room curtain and pulled it down while a high-profile politician had at least five grand worth of blow on the table, and an extremely young male blowing him. But that wasn't the worst of it. In a gentleman's club owned by an outlaw biker club, the one thing you don't do is mess with a man's ride. Leaning on Destroyer's Harley as she fixed a buckle on her shoe, her belt scratched his tank. The tank design was ruined.

She'll be paying that debt in blowjobs for months to come…or longer.

Shaking the last martini I need for a party of ten and laying it on the tray, I call over my best friend, and the woman I depend on the most. She's cocky, can bend any of these men to her will with the flick of her middle finger, and she's the President of The Four Horsemen's sister. "Jazzy."

Slapping Death on the shoulder in a playful but heavy way, Jazzy smiles my way. That is, until she looks toward Crystal.

Snapping up the drinks I've created, she narrows her eyes. "What's BI doing now?" She's refering to Crystal by her nickname—Blunt Instrument.

"I have her cleaning up. I'm hoping it's safer." I gave her the job of filling the dishwasher with the empties…Jesus fuckin' hell! Her tits are hanging out the front of her low-cut dress. "Crystal, your nipples are out," I state rather monotone, rolling my eyes.

Stopping to look down, she giggles. Her high-pitched sound grates on my nerves. "Sorry," she mumbles, wiggling the top seam to jostle her boobs back inside. She's so pressed into that minidress, that if she sneezed, she'd blow a seam. Even adjusting her tits is trying the material's limits.

She's not sorry. Not in the least.

I honestly wish she was better at this. We really need the help. Cursing under my breath, I look down the bar to Death, the president of his club and owner of Humble. He sits at the end closest to Crystal, eyeing the whole interaction with his VP, Curse. Neither of them will do anything about it.

They love watching me lose my shit. There are rules at the bar—*my rules*.

As the lone night bartender at the Humble Gentlemen's Club, I'm the boss behind the bar. No one touches my liquor, no one pours the draft, and if I don't give permission, you don't step behind. This is my domain.

I create the concoctions. I rule the world of liquid.

Sure, I do the usual, but this exclusive club gives me full reign to design concoctions as I please.

Turning my attention back to my work, I grab up my lighter and set the drinks I placed on Jazzy's tray aflame. With pink and blue goo floating within—like cum drizzled in a glass of water—it's erotic to the eyes. Plus, it tastes amazing. I call it, *To the Last Drop.*

"Thanks, babe." Grasping her tray carefully, Jazzy air kisses me as she walks off to serve her table. Hearing a loud clang, I turn, knowing exactly where it came from.

The fucking menace in a minidress.

Blowing out a hot breath, I grind my teeth together, almost afraid to look as another crash occurs. Spinning slowly, I peek out from under my narrowed brow, and the view is exactly as I expected. Ass in the air, glasses strewn on the floor, and Crystal attempting to pick them up. Her nine-inch heels deter her from bending low, the dress straining against her motion…and I can see she's not wearing panties.

"Death, come on. Do something about this." He smiles and shrugs. The only reason she's still here is because of the debt to Destroyer.

"So you won't do something?" I ask darkly.

He smiles sinisterly.

Fine! Make me the asshole.

Turning heel, I walk toward the disaster. "Stop. Whore on a Harley! Stop, Crystal!"

Her dress and heels make it awkward as she attempts to rise. It's painful to watch.

Holding out a hand, I help her stand. "Crystal—"

"I'm so sorry, Oubliette. I'm so sorry," she interrupts. Lifting a broken martini glass, Crystal turns my way with tears pouring down her face.

Those tears worked the first week, but not now. "Crystal, I've had enough. I can't have you back here."

"But I need this job!" She's sobbing so harshly, snot bubbles are coming out of her nose. "Please. I'll do anything, Oubliette."

Don't I know it.

"It doesn't matter. I can't have you here." Turning from her, I grab up a few of the glasses that didn't get damaged and set them on the bar in front of Death. Clearing his throat, he turns away.

His answer is no.

Fine. I'm firing her ass.

"Grab your stuff from the back, Crystal. I'll bring you your final pay."

CHAPTER 6

Oubliette

I left no room for argument. Crystal had her last chance. Death didn't want to do anything about her, and I had to be the bad guy. I hate that.

I might seem harsh, but it bothers me to be nasty to her.

Years ago, I needed a hand up too, and Death gave it to me. My parents had died in a car wreck when I was little, leaving myself and my brother as orphans. He was old enough to care for me, but I wanted to earn my own way—proving I could do things for myself. I wanted my parents to be proud of the girl I'd became—strong, resilient, take no shit. That I could stand on my own two feet.

At first, after completing university, I had no idea what to do with my degree in chemistry. I had a hard time finding a position in labs, and unless I had a minor in medical, I wasn't getting anywhere in this town. Yeah, I could move, but I won't leave my brother. Grady is all I have. Plus, he's a work whore and his girlfriend's an ass. So I'm here for moral support, and to be a gentle reminder that women can be lovely, not money grubby whores like Cammi.

Am I catty? Yes. I've never liked her.

Anyway. There was a position listed on an online site I frequent, of a company that was looking for a bartender. They offered a great pay schedule and awesome hours. That, I figured, gave me the ability to use my degree in a creative way. Six years later, I'm still the head bartender at the best gentleman's club in Anaheim. It may be owned by one of the most notorious motorcycle clubs in the area, but I do my job.

I hear it.

I see it.

I stay out of it.

Not my business.

Booze *is* my business, and getting patrons drunk. Without them drunk, they don't spend money, and I need them to spend money. The tips keep me in my life of semi-luxury.

"What the hell happened?" Jazzy asks, coming back from the VIP.

I'm still picking up shards as I tell her, "BI happened." Wiping the counter down and tossing glass shards in the bin, I'm careful not to get cut.

Tossing her tray onto the other empty ones, she shoves her way in beside me. "Let me help."

Jazzy is a few years older, colorfully tatted from wrist to neck on both arms. She's skinnier than me, has pixie chocolate hair, and a can-do attitude that helps me in times like this. She perks me up when I think I don't want it.

"Where'd she go? Why isn't she cleaning this, the fucking menace?"

Throwing out the towel, I bend down. "Because I fired her." Grabbing a shot glass with a huge chunk out of it, I toss it in the trash with the rest.

"'Bout time. Damn, woman." Tapping me on the shoulder, she smiles, showing her near perfect teeth. "You held out way longer than I would have."

Three weeks was two weeks, five days, and six hours too long.

Washing my hands up and surveying the damage, I start around the bar. "Watch the front for a bit? I promised I'd bring her last pay."

"Got it. Go deal with BI."

Walking to the back, the sounds of the thumping base and glass rattling treble dies off. Passing the stripper hall—which deviates off the main bar, is where Trigger stands guard with Radish, his service dog. I give him a smile.

He doesn't talk much, so I stopped trying months ago. PTSD left him with triggers, and conversations are nonexistent. I leave him, he leaves me. It's a mutual quiet.

Slipping by and working my way to our locker area, I notice it's excessively quiet. That in itself is surprising. That girl is a train wreck no matter where she goes, and her silence leaves me fearful. Walking in, I find the room empty. I check the shower and bathroom section, only to find them empty too.

"Fuck. Where'd that kid go?"

Pushing in the doors on each stall, Crystal is nowhere to be seen. Stepping back to the lockers, I check hers. The door is unlocked and her things are still inside. Even her phone. No law-abiding woman leaves her phone.

"Crystal?" I call out tentatively.

No reply.

Stepping into the hall, I make my way back toward Trigger, where he and Radish are just as I'd left them. "Did Crystal come back here?"

"Yeah, 'bout fifteen minutes ago."

"Did she come out?"

"Nah." Turning away from me, he doesn't leave any room for conversation. Honestly,

we're not his issue. The strippers are his to pro-
tect, and neither Crystal or I are a threat.

Deciding to recheck the room once more
and finding that she is indeed not inside, I walk
farther down the hall to the exit.

Humble is a four-story club that resides
near the sport's minded district. We do have a
fire escape that empties out to the street level
alley, and noticing the door is slightly ajar, with
a bright pink sequined heel holding it, I know
I've located Crystal.

But why is she out here?

Pulling out the heel, I slide the pin into the
push handle, which is used for keeping the door
unlocked, and shoulder it slightly.

"Lost your job? You *lost* your job!" A dark
voice snaps. "Did I not tell you what the consequences were?"

"Yes," Crystal answers. "You did, Bracken.
You warned me." Her words are strangled and
tight. She's afraid of this man. I can't quite see
them from here, hiding behind the door, and
they sound close enough that if I open it too far,
they'll see me. I don't need the heat, especially
for the likes of Crystal…but if he puts a hand on
her, I might have to grab one of the Horsemen.
Where we are down this hall to the alley though,

it'll be hard for them to know anything's going on. Even Trigger is too far away.

"I'm sorry, Bracken. I am."

"Sorry doesn't get me intel, Sis. Sorry doesn't get the info I need on the Horsemen, now does it?"

Shifting the door quietly, I look around the edge. It's nightfall, and even with the alley lights on, I should be hidden enough. Up against the wall, an arm at her throat, Crystal cries. Her back is ramrod straight as she tries to keep him from kinking her airway, all while standing on one shoe. I feel her pain.

Fuck. Do I close the door and try to grab Trigger or Death? Or do I interrupt them and hope he'll let her go when he's found out?

Figuring the latter, I push the door open.

"Crystal, you okay?" I ask, narrowing my eyes at the man.

He puts more pressure on her neck, forcing her to stretch out to breathe. "This isn't your business, cunt. Go back inside."

Crossing my arms, showing no fear, I scowl back. "Leave before I call the guys out here to deal with you. They don't take kindly to women being harmed in their employ."

He laughs. "Employed? Really? Crystal here was telling me you'd just fired her. Or was that a lie?" Punching her in the stomach, hard, Crystal coughs. Fighting for air as the man holds her up, she's clearly in over her head. I think I am too.

Pulling the door back, I move to yell for Trigger.

Taking a gun from his waistband, he points it at me. "Don't." Clicking the safety off, he growls, "Actually, do. I dare you. I'm looking forward to killing someone tonight."

I nod.

"Good." He smiles, and it's frightening. "You're smarter than you look, and smarter than *she* gave you credit for. Now, pull the door shut." He swings the gun, waving it back and forth.

Stepping out, leaving the door unlocked, I let it close behind me. Taking in his appearance, cataloging him for the retell, I consider every minute detail. Black pant suit with a well-tailored jacket, dark gray in tone. The shirt he's wearing is a muted blue, paired with a dark gray and a blue speckled tie. The outfit is clean, precise, and pricey. His skin is a dark mocha, no visible scars, and a perfected shave. He's meticulous in his appearance.

"Come on down. Let me see you better." He motions for me to move down the stairs.

I move slowly. Thankfully, concentrating on me causes him to release his hold on Crystal. I'll remember that asshole's name. When this is over, I'll relay all the details to Death. This bastard better know how to run. No one hurts women—Humble club rules, not including the Four Horsemen club rules. Club whores, old ladies, women in their employ, patrons, and family aren't to be harmed.

Gasping for air, leaning on her knees and choking back sobs, Crystal pulls off her other heel. Standing flat footed in the dingy alley, Crystal is still on alert, but slightly relaxed. If I were her, I'd have become the best one-heeled runner I could.

"So, let's get to know each other, shall we?" He glares as I stop at the bottom stair beside Crystal.

"I'm none of your concern," I sneer.

His brilliant white teeth shine in the bright light of the alley; his dark skin starkly in contrast to his smile. "Do you think I'm some fuck? An idiot?" Looking to Crystal, he raises his chin. "She's told me all about you, *Oubliette*." Stepping closer to me, I feel the heat of him as he closes in on my space. "You're the cunt that runs the bar. You hold the boys' balls in your back pocket. You know more about that club and those fucks than my sister could ever find out." A glint of mischief lights his eyes, and without warning, he fires his gun in her direction.

Striking fast, the bullet slips cleanly through her forehead, lodging itself in the brick behind her, as I'm splattered in blood and brain matter. Still looking to me, Crystal's eyes widen in surprise. Shocked by the whole thing, I don't react as her body slumps to the ground.

"That was unfortunate, wasn't it?" Bracken states, placing the gun in my direction. "Now, if you don't wish to have the same fate, what say you follow me." Indicating with the muzzle of the gun for me to move, he points down the alley.

I don't move. Grasping my arm, he drags me over the Crystal's dead body—a woman he called his sister. I'm beyond afraid.

"Fate calls, Oubliette."

Dragging me away, I don't argue, I don't speak. I stare at that gun pointed in my direction and wonder what the hell I need to do to get out of this.

CHAPTER 7

<u>Oubliette</u>

Rounding the alley, the whole district is quiet—hollow and devoid of humanity.

As we walk along, Bracken's gun is firmly resting on the naked space in the middle of my back. I'd stupidly worn a light top with the back open, and it's March. My coat is back at the club. I'm freezing, but as my adrenaline is pumping from this interaction, I'm numb. My senses note it, sure, but my mind isn't processing it. I only process the dead young girl at the back of my work. She died at the hands of the monster that's leading me away.

Approaching a black sedan, Bracken pops open the back door. "Get in," he snaps.

I don't move. I know that if I get in, I lose all control. I lose the chance to run. So I stand still, defying him.

"I won't ask nicely again. Get in, Oubliette." Pushing the muzzle tighter against my skin, I still feel the heat of its last kill. I have no choice. There's no one around to save me. No one to hear my cries or pleas.

He had no qualms in killing Crystal.

I mean, I'm less to him than her. *She* he called family. Maybe as I hop in, I can sneak out the other side.

Moving into the back seat, I sit and pull my heels off quickly. Sliding to the other side of the leather, I try the door.

Locked. "Fuck," I silently curse.

Jumping in beside me, Bracken closes the door with a thunk, then shifts forward to tap the driver on the shoulder. "Change of plans. Head out to the warehouse."

Starting the car and shifting it into gear, the driver pulls away. I watch as we leave the club and the protection the Horsemen.

Being the mouthpiece I am, being quiet isn't in my nature. It should be, but it's not. Not when I saw something that needed to be asked. "Why did you kill her? You called her your sister."

I don't see the resemblance. With her long, blonde, straight hair, bright oversized blue eyes that are now closed for good, he is a total contrast. Bracken is a good looking black man, but I can't see beauty in him. Evil has no beauty. Even with his wide shoulders, thick muscular chest, and deep brown eyes that have abysmal depths, it shows his madness. They glint with mischief.

He shrugs his shoulders. "She meant nothing to me. Crystal was nothing more than a tool for the job I needed done. She's dead. So what? The best thing she ever did was bring me you." Reaching out a hand to touch me, I shudder and shy away from his touch. "I won't harm you. That's not my job. I need you for information. After that, you're someone else's problem."

Confused by what he means, mainly because I have a high expectation of my death at the hands of this man, I can't fathom why I'm important. And the last thing I want is his attention.

Watching as we weave away from the city center, turning away from the cleaner parts of town to the dingy areas, I attempt to track our course.

"I know what you're thinking, and it won't work," Bracken huffs. Typing away on his phone, texting someone, he's not interested in me at the moment. Resting comfortably back against the supple leather, he's unafraid of me trying to plot our route. He knows something and it makes him complacent.

I can use that.

"What am I doing?" I ask, trying to seem at ease with the circumstances.

"You're trying to figure out where we are and where we're going. It won't do you any good. Soon, nothing will matter, Oubliette." Laying his gun beside him on the far end of the leather bench, he reclines peacefully.

I'm not a threat. Against his madness and that gun, it's true. I'm not a threat at all.

Not resigning myself to my fate, I snap back, "Why is that, Bracken?"

"Because you belong to us now."

CHAPTER 8

Busta

I met with the Four Horsemen's pres, Death, just under an hour ago. Now, sitting across the street from their club, Humble, in a little bar, going over all the points I need to tell the club at church, I'm enjoying a beer or two before I head back.

The Horsemen are a small club that deal in drugs and is known for their strip clubs. They keep to themselves, which has always been fine by me. Though, with our runs turning deadly, it's caused us to close ranks and to look into the clubs that we have weak relationships with. That includes the Four Horsemen, The Heartless Bastards, and the Restless Souls. We all have clubs within an hour of each other, but we've ran different businesses—never crossing. Never bothering with each other.

I fucking hate being here.

I hate the people and the atmosphere of Anaheim. Everything about it is set up to piss me off. I want to be at home. Though being the Enforcer, I do this type of work all the time by sussing out the enemies and destroying the threat. My decisions can play a key role in the changes, or my arrow can bring down those who fight us. There are times I hate it, but I'm damn good at it. Hell, most days I wonder where I begin and the club ends. Where the lies end and the truth starts. If I was asked, I might muddle things up in the telling.

The meeting went well enough, but it was the woman mixing the drinks that truly caught my attention. She was drop-dead gorgeous. Good size hips for holding, the perfect set of tits, and golden hair long enough to ponytail hold when you ride her from behind.

That ass wasn't what attracted me to her. Her take-no-shit attitude did.

Getting a text from True, I set down my beer.

True: Need you now. Warehouse three, wharf nine.

Me: I met with Death.

True: Tell me later. Warehouse. Now.

Not much of a choice when he puts it like that. Fuck. Guess that means I'm back on the bike.

Stepping into the light of day, I leave the bar with a heavy heart. Going out to my bike, I check the address and head out to our warehouses in Long Beach. I told them once I'd never babysit or help package up the merchandise, and I was pretty fuckin' serious. DG gave me an ultimatum then, that I could stay out of the flesh as long as I did what they needed done between the clubs. True commanding I go there, a man who knows the deal, is breaking and making his own rules. True could drive me out over this one request.

He has a singular job for me.

Those normally mean my ass cleaning up blood and gore, but the warehouse doesn't usually include that. Those *housed* there waiting for transport are usually too valuable.

Starting my custom, I stroke the tank. It's a bobber. I'd taken a vintage seventies Fat Bob, stripped it down, pulled all the shit off that I didn't need or want and trimmed the fat. The modification of the ape hangers suits me just fine. I'd commissioned this kid at our club to re-do the artwork. He'd painstakingly recreated what I'd seen on my stepdad's bike; the fearless magenta woman that haunts my dreams. Her eyes blaze, banked by a wildfire, with discarded bones stacked under her heels—all as she crushes them in defeat. The powerful and immortal skeletal shield maiden sings to me. She's haunted me for years. I even had her tattooed on my leg.

Traveling away from the compound, I head out to the docks. Arriving a short while later, I meet up with Nock in the parking lot, just as True pulls up in a car.

"How'd it go?" Carter asks. A few inches shorter than me, Carter smacks me on the shoulder as I stand before him. His road name, Nock, is based on how fast he can load and shoot an arrow.

That's the thing with the Bows; everything has to do with a bow or arrow in some way. *Blessed is the Arrow that Strikes True.* We're expert marksmen. We can take down a hit from fucking yards away. If you want to be a Bow, you have to best either True or his twin brother, Strike. That was the rule. Nock isn't the best shot, but he can knock off more in a minute than anyone else, always hitting his target. He and True are as thick as thieves. They grew up in the club together, learned how to fuck together with the same whore, killed their first runner together, and were patched in at the same time. They're closer than brothers, more than True and his identical twin. Both have the same tendencies, the same career ambitions, and the same taste in women.

They're fucked.

Strike doesn't even come around the club. He disowned his family for the church, becoming a man of the cloth. I personally think he escaped. I guess you could say I *envy* his ass in a way. He left the life, he's on the straight and narrow path now. I wish I was the same. The Bows' are far from perfect, but I wonder how great this club could be if we were cleaner?

Climbing off my bike, laying my helmet on the seat, I clasp Nock's hand in a heavy shake. "How was the ride?" It's a Friday. Traffic is always bad at this time of the week.

His sinister and morbid grin reminds me of his tastes in women—or tastes *for* women. He loves to cause them pain. Having him here at the shipping depot could be costly. Yeah, he's a joker, but only when it comes to anything *not* related to pussy and ass.

"It was fine. You know why I'm here?" I ask him.

He shakes his head. "Nah. I'm just meeting True. We're going out to some club."

"Dancing? Really?" I snicker.

"Nah. We're meeting with a snitch from Alta."

Who could they be meeting?

As Enforcer, it's my job to give them backup. Before I can ask, though, stepping out of a sleek limo, dressed to the nines, with no cut or colors, True looks like an investment banker. He looks fucking rich. No visible tattoos, no jeans, his hair freshly shaved, his beard trimmed low, and in a gray-black suit. Very gangster. Very mobster. Wherever it is they're going, it's high-end.

"I have a job for you, Busta." Bending low, he looks in the limo, then turns back to me. "Take good care of it."

Looking inside the back seat, I see the woman from the Humble Club—the bartender. I'm babysitting *her?* I'm to keep her company? I both relish and despise the position. I hate the flesh trade we deal in. I hate the holding cells. I hate that he's running off to a meet without proper backup. I hate that she's mine to watch over. But I'll do as I'm told because I'm a good soldier. Because it's my fucking job.

As True and Nock take off in the car, leaving her with me, I'm unsure of how I'm going to keep my fucking hands to myself. I'd rather rope my fingers through that hair and fuck her ten ways to Sunday.

If she's up for it.

Damn, I hope she is.

CHAPTER 9

<u>Oubliette</u>

After an hour's drive, we pull up to an abandoned building by the ocean. I've been biding my time. My best chance is to wait him out. All I can do is hope that he slips up.

Maybe not him directly, but he'll ask someone to do something with me and they'll fuck up. They'll forget to lock a door, they'll miss that there's a window big enough for my little ass to squirm through, or a cell phone will be on a table nearby that I can pilfer and use discreetly.

"Don't worry, Oubliette," Bracken states, sounding bored.

"I'm not worried."

Untrue. I'm totally freaking out.

As the car stops and the door to the building beside us opens up, I watch with wild fear. Two men—no, more like mountains with chest hair, traverse the distance to us in under three steps each.

I'm still plotting my escape, but I'm less confident now.

With the door to the car swinging wide, Bracken steps out, talking directly to them. "Took a turn."

Bending low, looking inside, one of them smiles. "Hey, lovely." His voice is dark and hints at mischief, but his smile is genuinely creepy. "Who the fuck is she?"

"She's our *in* to the Horsemen intel," I hear Bracken inform him.

Not reacting to the comment, I stay curled up in the corner. I won't give them the satisfaction of my fear.

"What about Crystal?" His voice is argumentative, questioning. He's concerned.

"Crystal's a dead end. Oubliette here is a wealth of information." Seeing Bracken's shadow move, he turns toward the back of the car, stepping to the other side where I'm hiding. Popping the door, I shuttle across to the middle.

"Let's go, Oubliette. You know what happens when I don't think you're important anymore. I'd hate to see that sexy body with a new hole courtesy of my 9 mil."

Fuck. I do know.

Deciding to take my chances with the men on the other side, I slide across the seat to the far side—away from Bracken—and step out. Feeling intimidated by the sheer size of these two hulking men, I memorize them too. This info will be important for the Horsemen.

The first one, the one with the big smile that speaks of pain, has broad shoulders a slight paunch to his gut—too much beer and fatty foods—a well kept beard, and shorn short hair. His leather cut says Nock, Broken Bows, San Bernardino's Finest, The One. He also has the eight ball and one percent patches with four consecutive year tags. Tags I've seen before at the Horsemen club.

"Thought we were the safer bet?" he crows, feeling confident.

Working at Humble, it's a steady flow of MC cuts and reading rockers. Broken Bows is one that I'd seen earlier on the man before me. He doesn't smile. His permanent scowl seems stuck—frozen to his features. Narrowing his eyes, even from this distance, and with the street light behind him, I can see the bright green shimmering. They're electric.

His face is rigid, tight, and without mirth. Where there should be laugh lines, he has none. His bright green eyes are searching, but they don't give anything away. He's a closed book.

Him I'm afraid of.

With his size and stature, he's even bigger than the first guy. At least six five, two hundred plus pounds—probably closer to three—and a beard to rival any I've seen.

Almost all the local clubs are friendly with the Horsemen, so who are these guys? And San Bernardino is at least an hour away in good traffic, if there was ever good traffic in Los Angeles cities.

Now that I'm out of the car, my original assessment was spot on. They're all very intimidating. Stepping in front of them, shoeless, because I ditched them in the car, I'm left staring up at the green-eyed man. Checking out his cut, taking in the details, I memorize it. *San Bernardino Broken Bows, The One* is neatly stitched in on black and white patches, with the same one percent.

His name is Busta.

His tag states he's the Enforcer. Makes sense. I'm sure he could destroy me in moments. If he smacked me, I'd soar across the parking lot.

Walking silently over to where I am, Bracken taps my shoulder, jolting me out of my perusal.

"Oubliette." He raises my discarded black pumps. "Your shoes. I wouldn't want you to walk without them. It's rather nasty in there."

Oh, please. I won't thank him, and putting them on constitutes a lack of opportunity to run away. No respectful woman can run in heels. That only happens in movies.

Turning to the smug guy, Bracken asks, "Nock, did you have any issues with the supplies? Were they cooperative?"

"Haven't even lifted a lid." He looks to me. "She going to the same place?"

Shrugging his shoulders nonchalantly, Bracken smiles and reaches to play with my hair. I take a step back. "Undecided. For now, she's a guest of the Bows. Let's see if Oubliette can be cooperative."

"Fuck you, Bracken," I spit out. "The last thing I want to be is cooperative."

Venturing a look around the area, behind the big guy, I see an opening between the buildings. We're close enough, that if I could get a good running start, I should be able to get away. It's not a big space, so the two big bikers won't have a chance to follow me. Bracken, though, he could contend if he were wearing runners instead of loafers.

Laughing, Nock claps his hands together. "Jesus fuckin' Christ, True! That's a good one. How often does someone other than Pres call you that?"

"Shut your trap, *Carter*," Bracken snaps back, before raising his gun to Carter's temple. "I dare you. Oh, brother, I dare your ass." He's deathly serious.

Lifting his hands in defeat, Carter scowls, but he's not who I'm watching. It's Busta. With his left hand resting on the crook of his back, I know he's palming his weapon. He's unhappy with the turn of events.

Holstering his gun, he turns to me. "Bracken's my name, sweetheart. But I'm the VP of the Broken Bows. My name is True. That's how you'll address me from now on." He then turns his sights on Carter. "You'd do good to remember that."

Right now, I need a way out.

Right now, I should be serving drinks.

Right now, I should be walking Crystal out with her last paycheck in hand and wishing her good luck.

Right now, I should be laughing it up with Jazzy and harassing Death for his lack of balls for dealing with the Crystal issue, but no. I'm dealing with this.

"You want her in the back room then?" Busta asks, ignoring the cock posturing.

Jesus, his voice is angelic. It's melodic, deep, growly, and panty-melting, but not what I should be concentrating on. I *should* be worrying about the point that the Broken Bows have taken me hostage.

They're the enemy.

He's the enemy.

This is a moment I wish I could restart. I would've gone home, drank myself into oblivion and worried about Crystal's blundering for another day.

Clearing my mind of the recent situation with Crystal and Bracken, I concentrate on the matter at hand, which is Busta, and that he's here to apparently babysit me.

Why?

Why are we here? The wharf warehouses aren't really a great MC club spot. Too much heat—or at least I've heard that around the club in conversations.

Opening the car door, True steps in. "She's yours to watch until I need to ask her questions about the Horsemen. We need further intel about their territory, and I think our *friend* Oubliette can give us that. Keep her safe, brother."

Nodding his head to True, Busta steps closer to me, searing me with those electric eyes. "She won't be going anywhere. Will you, Oubliette?"

Choking on the opportunity to reply crassly, I stay silent.

Silence will piss them off.

Silence will be what will give me my freedom.

CHAPTER 10

Oubliette

"Come on," Busta says as True drives off with the other guy, Nock. He doesn't touch me, he doesn't grab me by the arm, but he leaves no room for me to choose otherwise. I'm going where he says *because* he says it.

Still gripping my heels tightly, I contemplate using them as a weapon. Then I think twice about it and remember his neatly tucked away gun in his backside. I didn't see it. I didn't need to. I knew it was there by the instinctive move he made when True held a gun at Nock.

Popping the heavy metal door to the building, I notice it isn't locked. No key was necessary and no passcode pad was used. Trusting bikers? Highly fucking unlikely. He's not afraid of anyone wanting in.

He stands to the side. "After you, but I suggest the shoes. Like True said, I wouldn't walk barefoot in here."

Blowing out a hot breath, I resign myself to his recommendation. Placing each shoe on slowly, I come closer to Busta's face—small scars that hint to teenage acne, a small cross mark near his ear, and a square jaw.

"Ready now? Done checking me out, sweetheart?"

I'm not shocked that he noticed, so I tell him the truth. "Nope. Making sure I have you right for the police sketch artist."

Reaching out, gripping my hand gently, he pulls it toward his cock. "Don't forget this. It's my best feature. We don't want them missing this," he taunts, his voice thick with tension.

Yanking my hand back quickly, I instinctively smack his face. "Don't presume I want to know you."

There's a light in his eyes as he licks the edge of his lip, tasting blood. "After you, Princess."

Slightly surprised he didn't retaliate—he is an outlaw biker after all—I step into the darkened building. There are no windows, no source of light, and not even emergency exit signs to note the door we're entering. As Busta shuts the door, that faint light from outside is gone. "Stand here," he growls.

I hear him step away, his heavy feet making a melodic sound as he lifts them one by one. He walks off a distance. Turning, I try the door we'd come through, but it won't open. It's locked. Pulling on it a few times, it rattles but doesn't budge.

What the fuck!

"It won't open without a code," Busta calls out from far away. Still unable to adjust my eyes to the space, I'm unsure of what I'd walk or fall into. Placing my shoes on and tapping my heels on the floor, the sound echoes. Taking small steps, I shift along, reaching out with my hands. When they connect with metal tubes, solid and thick, I feel around it. Evenly spaced, each are about the span of my hand apart. Continuous and consistent, I follow them, tapping the floor and moving my hands one over the other. I don't know how far I've moved, but I've felt at least ten of those tubes.

"Close your eyes, Oubliette," Busta calls out loudly, his voice echoing off the walls.

"No!" I yell back. "Fuck you, Busta! Fuck you!" Still walking in the same direction, I continue. I'm hoping this slow progression will gain me a chance at freedom, but it's highly unlikely.

"Oubliette, close your eyes. Trust me. You won't like the outcome otherwise." I hate that he can state my name and it sounds alluring. I hate that he sounds as if he's trying to gain my trust and lessen my fear. I hate everything about him right now. "Last warning."

"Kiss my ass!" I scream out as a blinding light shocks my senses I cover my eyes with the palms of my hands, seeing stars. I feel as if I'd just stared directly into the sun. Attempting to pull my hands away, the pain of the brightness is headache inducing. "Fuck," I mutter.

I can hear Busta's feet as he moves, and I know he's coming my way. Pulling my hands away from my face and keeping my eyes closed, I continue along the path. Hoping to find a doorway or a hiding place, I shudder at the thought of what he has in store.

"Oubliette," he says softly as he comes close. "You know, I'll bet you're called something else by friends, Princess. Oubliette sounds like a mouthful."

With my eyes still closed, I continue moving, cursing under my breath, "I'm not your friend." I'm not about to give away my location if I'm hidden. Attempting to open my eyes again, the starry feeling is gone, but left in its wake are halos.

"Oubliette." Hearing him closer, I speed up.

"Shit, shit, shit, shit," I curse and curse as I run my hands along the poles as fast as my heels can click to confirm the floor—or lack thereof.

There has to be another way out.

Blinking my eyes over and over, the halo dissipates and the poles come into focus.

Bars.

Stopping dead in my tracks, I look the length of the distance I've covered and where I intend to go.

It's all bars.

Clearing the last of my night blindness, the fear and dread of what I'm seeing becomes fully visible.

"What the fuck?" I mutter in disgust. From one end to the other, there are cages…full of women and girls.

As I stand there aghast, from behind me, his dark voice sends a chill up my spine.

"Hello, Oubliette."

CHAPTER 11

Oubliette

Stumbling on the thoughts that cross my mind, I reel with the image before me. Cage upon cage, women and girls of all ages, some as young as ten I'd bet, are all huddled in cages. There's no nationality here, no rhyme or reason to their captivity, and they're all deeply frightened souls. You can tell those that have been here for days, weeks, or months. Some you can see have lost all hope.

"Are you ready to follow me now, Oubliette?" His dark tone is focused on me as I process the depths of this depravity.

"Who are they? Why are they here?" I ask softly. My voice has escaped me, leaving me with only a squeak.

"They're someones and no-ones. They're those who owe a debt, or are a debt who is owed. You're not one of them. Not yet." Holding out his hand, asking me to take it, I look into those deep green pools. I thought they were enticing and beautiful, but now all I see is an abysmal ocean floor. Dark, tainted, unfriendly and unaware of how soulless he's become. If he can see this and not react, he's dead inside.

Shaking from the shock of it, I can't move. I can't process it as I stare into the eyes of women who are broken and defeated. I'm not stupid, I know the world has its underbelly and darkened corners. I mean, I work for an outlaw MC for fuck's sake, but this is something I never imagined I'd see.

"Oubliette?" He takes my chin and forces me to look up at him. "Come on. Let me take you away from this." How chivalrous.

When I don't move, he tries to direct me.

"Don't," I whisper. When he tries again, I say it with more force and conviction. "Don't touch me."

Pulling his hand back, he drops it at his side. "How about I make you a deal then?"

Unsure of where he's going, I listen.

"For every time you do as I ask, giving up a piece of information, I'll release one person of your choosing." Before I can answer, he adds, "But the one person cannot be you."

Taken aback, I pause.

How dare he think that little of me!

Steaming pissed at his audacity, I change course and focus my energy on him. "You don't know me, yet you already assume that I'd choose myself first over that of these desperate women and girls." Poking him in the chest, I push against him. "You think I'd care about myself more than them? They look starved. Most probably haven't seen sunshine in months, and don't even get me started on a bath, and you think I'd rather leave here *first*?"

"Isn't that what you were doing? Trying to find a way out?" he asks calmly.

"Yes! Yes I was. Until you flicked the switch and brought them to my attention."

He smiles, just enough that it can be seen through his beard. I'm even more annoyed. "Why are you smiling?" I growl out.

As fast as it appeared, it vanishes. "I don't smile." Shaking it off and turning toward where he came from, he asks again, "Do we have a deal, Obi?"

"My name is Oubliette, *Busta*." Fuck, he's pissing me off. "And what kind of road name is Busta anyway?"

Crossing his arms, he growls, "It's mine. Now, do we have a deal?"

Crossing my arms, I stare him down. "Do I have a choice?"

He begins cracking the kinks out of his neck, looking bored. "Nope. I hold all the cards if you want to help them."

Looking back at the women again, the children huddled and afraid, I straighten my back. "Lead on then."

Busta reaches to grasp my hand, and I pull back fast. "Don't touch me," I snap once more.

He smiles again, but this time it reaches his eyes. "I won't until you give me permission."

CHAPTER 12

<u>Oubliette</u>

Leading the way past cage after cage, the women look to me, imploring, hoping I'm their savior. Not yet. But I'll find a way if I can.

I've yet to see a window in this vast space, and the area smells of defeat. It's musty. I doubt that they've even had proper hygiene needs met in such conditions.

I've seen dogs in better care than this.

"Why?" I ask him again.

"It's what we do. The Bows traffic in merchandise. They're merchandise." He points to the sad sacks in the cages.

"That's callous," I say, without thinking it through.

Stopping dead in his tracks, Busta turns to me. "Yes, it is." He slaps his hand against his chest, over his 1% marker. "You work with the Four Horsemen. You know what it means, don't you, Obi?"

I nod at his harsh tone. "It says one percent," I reply.

"Right. And that means I don't give a fuck. None of us do." Stepping closer to me than I find comfortable, I have to crane my neck upwards to make eye contact. "We're the scum. The assholes that don't give a shit about laws, you, your father, your sister, your cunt of a best friend—we don't care unless you're wearing one of these." Grasping his cut, he shakes it. "If I wanted to, I could put you over my knee, spank you until you cried out, then sink balls deep into your cunt." He narrows his eyes. "But I don't. Not because of some weak-minded deal I struck with you, but because I'm not a fucking rapist."

"Well that's a blessing, I guess. You either televise your attack and act like an angel, or you capture and sell off people without remorse. So you own one single decent moral; you don't rape. Not giving me much to trust, Busta."

Stopping, his eyes drill into me, looking with wonder that I'd speak the truth. Turning heel, he continues. "Those men and women that buy them, they're the scum. I'm just the handler, Oubliette." Not looking over his shoulder to see if I follow, I can hear the disappointment in his tone. He may act like he doesn't care, but his tone gives it away. He does.

As I continue behind him—albeit slightly damper in my panties than before. Even pissed off, he's hot and I reacted. Sure, my brother Grady says I have a thing for the bad boys, but my ideal bad boy isn't one who captures, contains, and trades women and children like hockey cards for a profit.

Working for the Four Horsemen for the last six years, I've seen a lot. And I mean *a lot.* I can't say that I've ignored it all, but I haven't turned a blind eye and thought that they were angels.

Did I think they could be involved in something like this? With the Broken Bows? Shit. I fucking hope not. It makes me sick to my stomach to think they could be.

Continuing our upward advance, being the mouthy bitch I am, I ask Busta more. I might as well gain info from him. "Are they a part of this too?"

"Who? The Horsemen?"

"Yeah. Are they?" I'm dreading the answer, but I figure it's better to know.

"Nah. They deal in drugs. Prostitutes aren't their thing. They're legit with their Humble Club. The girls are employed, not bought. All of them are on the up-and-up. The Horsemen like to kill fuckers slowly with their junk."

I'm not sure that I'm happier with that, but it's a small thing that eases my conscious about my employer.

Hitting the top of the stairs, it levels out to a large room with an even longer hallway. The area has one of those gangways that you see in movies that course the upper area of a warehouse. It stretches to the back, suspended over the area where we were below. Seeing it like this, it's worse. It's way worse. The size of this warehouse, the sheer volume of it, it must be three times that of the Humble Club. From end to end, it's nine by nine cages with no end in sight. Each one houses at least three to five women and girls.

"This is what hell looks like then," I whimper.

Coming up beside me, staring down at the destitute, his voice is soft as he replies with, "I'm not the devil, but I enforce his rules. And yes, this is what hell looks like, Obi." Placing his hand near mine, he softly brushes the edge of my pinky. "Do as you promised, and you'll relieve them of this hell. Well, at least for a few."

If only I could release them all. Considering the idea of pulling the gun out from his back while he's relaxed and not on guard about my intentions, I wonder if I could do it? Could I kill someone, all so I could save more lives?

One for the many? Now I understand that analogy. The only flaw in the plan is that he's definitely stronger, quicker, and he has more to lose if I succeed. Therefore, he's hungrier for it. Again, I decide it's best if I bide my time. I'll find a way to get free, and I swear on my own life that I will save these women.

Turning around, taking in the room, I find it's well supplied. There's a fridge, stove, micro-wave, three large couches, a big screen TV mounted on the wall, and two doorways that I assume lead off to a bathroom and a bedroom.

"So, where will I be jailed? Are one of those cages mine?" I ask it with cynicism, but truly, I'm hoping he says no. There's only so much I can take today after these events. Call it selfish, but I figure in there, with them, I have less of a chance to change their fate.

"No. The bedroom on the right is yours. There's a bed, a bathroom off the side of it, and no," he walks up to me as I case the joint, his answer is curt, "there are no weapons in the kitchen. Not unless you count plastic butter knives and a blender for protein shakes."

Looking down at my thin shift-like shirt, I ask, "And what do I do about this?" The skinny black jeans I'm wearing, and heels, are going to get rank after a day or two. I don't think he's expecting to leave here to grab a bag from home or go shopping. So I start considering the options afforded to me in sleepwear. "There's not a snowball's chance in hell that I'll sleep naked to conserve my clothing longer."

"You're fucking high maintenance, Obi."

"My name is Oubliette, not Obi. Only one person has been afforded the right to call me that, and he's seen me in diapers. If you want me to answer you, then address me by my full name." When the fuck did I grow balls the size of watermelons? Standing up to Busta could be my fucking funeral. Or maybe, it's that I have nothing left to lose.

I've been kidnapped by a biker gang, told that I'm a *guest*, which is bullshit, and I can only help out other captured women if I rat on the Four Horsemen.

Decisions, decisions.

Yeah. I don't have a great deal of choice. And when I'm free, I'm dead. There's no other way out of this. Death will come knocking and my fate will have been sealed.

Plunking himself down on the couch, grabbing up the remote and flicking to an action film, the loud crashes and bangs immediately engulf the space. "If you want to go to sleep, I think there's a few old tees in there you could wear."

Sure, I'll sleep. My mind won't be reeling for hours on end, and a thin piece of cotton will reassure me. "I'm good," I tell him, even though I'm totally on the edge of losing my shit.

Without looking my way, Busta hits the mute button. "Oubliette, I'm not gonna harm you. I'm not gonna attack you in your sleep."

"And I can trust you?"

Right?

He shrugs. "I guess we'll find out." Turning the volume back on, he dismisses me. "Good-night, Oubliette."

CHAPTER 13

Busta

My cock remembers her. It remembers her lovely hair, her fabulously thick hips, and that thin body that begs for my hands to touch every inch of it. And that mouth.

Jesus fucking Christ!

This woman will be the death of me. Her fucking attitude will cause me a coronary. I'll bust a blood vessel just trying to destress in the shower.

Avoid her, Lucius. Keep as far away as you can. That's what I keep telling myself. The way she tried to put me to ground with her words, I know she can hold her own against any with a flick of that tongue.

Her reaction to the merchandise—it cut me. I'd done everything I could to shut off my emotions about the job I do. About the pain I assist in. About the life I'm leading that's a total fucking lie.

This is the exact reason I avoid women in my life. I have no girlfriend—never have. They're all drama, damage inducing, heart crushing beasts. The club whores are one thing, as I can toss them away—use, abuse, and set loose. I have no care for an old lady. I'd look for love in a bottle before a woman's heart.

I like being alone. There's no secrets to worry about hiding, no unusual trips that could cause concern, and I can step out without question.

I have the one thing I need, the loyalty of my brothers. It's something I don't always feel I deserve, but I have it.

I'm a bastard, but there's so much more to it.

Watching her waltz off to the side bedroom, hearing the lock turn, I know she's expecting privacy and solitude after her abduction. I'll give her a bit to feel at ease, then we'll see.

Will she turn over on the Horsemen to save these women?

Will she break their trust?

Can I *trust* she's telling the truth?

And if she does turn over on them, do I have it in me to kill her for rolling on a club?

CHAPTER 14

Oubliette

Sleep? You fucking kidding me? It wasn't in the cards. My mind reeled.

Below, there are women in cages. In cages! There are children that wonder where their mommy or daddy are, and how they were so bad that they deserved this. They've heard their fate, I'm sure.

And I'm sleeping on a soft bed? No. I can't.

How these men—if they can be called that—could do this to countless humans over and over is unimaginable. I put them at the same level as puppy kickers, those who set cats on fire, or the sick fucks that thinks it's okay to rape their own child.

I may be stuck in here for now, but I will get out and save them *all*. Not one of them will be left here to their fate. I *will* free them.

I tore the room apart looking for an exit— silently of course. The windows in this room are too high. Even with the use of the bed and the lone stool that rests in the corner, there's no way I could reach the latch. I have no idea if there's something to catch my fall on the way down, and that's a big problem.

Checking the time on my watch, it's almost 7am. I've processed every scenario for so long that I've rode through the night. And Busta never came in. He didn't even break down the door. He didn't do anything against me. That alone surprises me.

With the sun rising through the dirty windows, I finally rise off the bed. Going to the bathroom and washing up, cleaning off my *work* makeup, I feel more human. I look super plain, but I don't think looking like I'm ready for the club will help me get out of here either.

Unlocking the door, I peek out of the room and see Busta asleep on the couch. Throughout the night, I could hear the television, and walking into the room, it's now off. Tiptoeing across the space, making my way to the edge of the railing, I look down at the sight before me. I'm looking for another exit—another way to escape this hell. I don't see one, but that doesn't mean there isn't one.

"Good morning," his growly voice says from behind me.

Jesus Christ!

I thought I was quiet, but he must have superhuman hearing skills and movements of a ninja. I thought he was still on the couch. Inspecting the man beside me, I'm stunned. He's beautiful. Busta at some point removed his leather cut and white tee, and he's now only wearing his low-slung jeans, dark tattoos and sun-kissed skin.

Stretching skyward, his jeans fall even lower, showcasing his V. A slight trail of hair delves below the beltline, showing his body is strong. He may be the scum of the earth, but his body is well cared for. If he were anyone else other than my jailor, I'd think he was sexy.

Slinging on his shirt, then his cut, he chirps, "You done inspecting me?"

I try to act nonchalant about it, but it doesn't matter. I might as well speak the truth. "You don't have a gut. I was just surprised."

"I look after myself. Should I not?"

I think I actually hurt his feelings.

I shrug. I honestly could care less about the minuscule feelings that this man has. I only want a way out. "I guess if you're catching runners all the time, it helps."

Shaking his head with distaste, he holsters his gun in his belt. "They don't run. Runners get bullets. Those move faster than I ever will."

Unsure of how to answer that, I stand straight and face off against him. "Is there food here? I'm starved."

"You always this pushy?"

I swore I wouldn't show fear. Not to him. Not to them. It won't do me any good to seem weak anyway. "It's not like I shouldn't be hungry. I never had dinner. It's been a long fucking night and I'm hungry. Can you blame me?"

His heavy boots clack on the floor as he moves with intent, stopping short of bumping me against the railing. Piercing me with those green eyes, Busta looks down. "You don't call the shots. You're not my old lady. You're not in charge, and I don't have to feed you. I can stuff your ass in a cage with them if you wanna keep trying my patience." Pointing below, his voice is menacing. "You best remember that."

"I work in a biker owned club. I see through you. I see the same in you as I do in them. You all think you're fucking tough ass men." I attempt to sidestep him, but he places a hand on the railing behind me. "You don't scare me, *Busta,*" I say in a condescending tone.

"Give me something," he grinds out.

"What? You lonely? Are you looking for sex?"

He laughs harshly. "Not from you. I don't need to fight for it, Oubliette."

"Then what do you want when you say *something?*"

"How do they move the drugs? Where's their warehouse? Who did they pay off? Are they working with Restless Souls? Did they help attack our run? Give me intel on the Horsemen, Obi."

Closing my mouth, I scowl. He can't think it's that easy, that I'd turn over on the Horsemen within the first twenty-four hours. Being starved is better than breaking their trust. That their trust was that easy to expel is a joke. I stand rigid and stiff, clasping my lips tightly.

"Nothing?" he growls. "Nothing's worth helping these women and showing me some good faith?"

Laughing out loud, I grip the railing tight as I square off with a man that should honestly scare the piss out of me. I won't beg, though. I won't say please. I won't fall apart for him because he growls low. I won't crash because he's honestly good looking. I'm stronger than you think, big guy. It'll take a ton more to break me.

Narrowing my gaze and staring at him, I smile. "Good luck."

"Fine. Let's try this then, shall we?"

Grasping me by the arm and pulling me toward the stairs, Busta drags me behind him. I don't beg for him to slow, even though I'm having a hard time keeping up. My bare feet are aching on the open grates, but I won't give him the satisfaction of my distress. As we reach the bottom, after Busta stomps down each stair harshly, he pulls me close. Turning me, flattening my face against the bars, he tucks his body in close to my back. "See them? See these broken fucks? Do you want that? Do you *want* me to shove you in there?" His hot breath on my neck as his chest heaves is rushed and thick. I don't speak, but I don't fight him either. Standing straight, not giving an inch of my fear to him, I let out a haughty breath, like I'm bored. Like he's not affecting me.

I won't give in.

I won't let him win.

He won't win in this war of strength.

"Do you see it?" Speaking low, his voice vibrates. "Their pain. Their anguish. Their disgust. They're reduced to a bucket for a bathroom and a concrete floor for a pillow. Do you want to be there? Tell me honestly, Obi."

Grinding my teeth, I war with the need to tell him off for the term of endearment that is reserved only for Grady—my sweet, investment banking, paper-pushing brother. Arguing the point that I've already told him he's not allowed to call me that won't fix it either. There's no use in it. It's what he wants. He *wants* me to fight him. I will. Otherwise, I'd be the same as these frightened souls. The crushed and desperate. I see that they've given in.

"Put me in there then, Busta, you big tough asshole," I spit out. Pushing my ass back against him, I shove him away in disgust. "Put me in the cage. See if I care."

Crushing me against the bars, his voice and tone is calm, yet dangerous. This close, his heat is hard to miss, so is his semi-erect cock pressing against the confines of his jeans as it rocks against my body. "I'm an asshole, am I? Did I bother you all night long? Did I break down the door? Did I stick my cock in your mouth and tell you to suck it? Did I force myself on you in any way, Obi?"

With my face tight in-between the bars, I yell out, "Stop calling me Obi! You don't have the right to call me that." I'm really starting to hate how he feels he can call me that at all. "My name is Oubliette. Say it. It's not hard, just a few extra syllables."

Pushing away from the bars and away from me, Busta gives me room to turn around. I swear he's enjoying this way too much.

"Oubliette. So testy about a name." Smiling, his eyes turn up as his lips do in a wide grin. "If I want to call you Obi, there's nothing you can do to stop me. Nothing." Reaching out a hand, he attempts to push my hair out of my face.

Lifting a hand on instinct, I slap it away and hit him hard across the face. If he wanted me steamed, he got it. I'm pissed off now.

"I'm not yours! You'll *never* call me that again."

With a dark and sinister glower, Busta bends down to my height. Face-to-face with me, he grinds out, "As you wish." Rising to his full height, he curls his lip up and reaches around my body. "I made you a deal and I'll stand by it. If you give me intel on the Horse-men, I'll release someone. I asked nicely, and you turned the first chance down."

With a click, I hear a resounding scrape across the floor. I don't dare take my eyes from his, but I'm curious, so I look. "Your accommo-dations." Pushing his form forward causes me to backup a step, allowing him to corral me into the open cage.

"You can ask for your meals to be prepared a certain way. You can ask for a shower, a toilet break, a moment of seclusion, but until you real-ize you're not in control, *this* will be your new home. Until you relent, my queen."

Taking a step back, Busta leaves the cage. Closing the door behind him, the scratch of the lock clicks once more. "Welcome to your castle."

With a smirk, he walks away.

CHAPTER 15

Oubliette

Yep. I'm an idiot. I tempted the lion and he caged me. Curling up on the floor, I take in the confines. There are stains on the floor from previous women in distress, a bucket without a handle, and nothing more. It's hell for whoever lived here before. It's not my hell yet, but it could be if I don't give him what he wants.

Sleep has been my only companion. The other women won't talk to me, and the children are too afraid.

Tromping up the stairs, I swear I heard him mutter, "She'll break me before I break her."

CHAPTER 16

Oubliette
Day Two

I have the sniffles. I hate that. I'm cold. I'm desperately in need of a pee, and I refuse to use the bucket that was supplied unless I truly have no other choice.

Busta has taken phone calls, and while I see him leaning over the edge as he speaks to them, I can't hear the conversation.

At one point, I watched him drink down a glass of something that looked milky and creamy. I felt my mouth water at the sight, and thought of giving in just for a taste. I don't ask for food and I won't beg him.

Turning, so that I can't see his face, I curl up in the corner, using my light shift of a shirt as a pillow. It's not much, but it helps.

Drifting off to sleep, I hope for rescue.

Waking up a few hours later, I find a glassful of that sweetness resting just inside my confines with a worn T-shirt. I haven't touched it. I won't give him the satisfaction.

Looking around, Busta is nowhere to be seen, but I know he placed it there.

I can't be expected to survive without food, and I've seen him dropping things at the doors of the other cages. Grabbing it up, downing it in heaping gulps, my stomach rebels against the intrusion after so long without, but I don't care. If I wish to fight him or someone else, I have to have my strength. I need my wits. No food equates to hysteria.

Looking up as I drink, I see him resting on that railing again, staring at me, fixed and imploring. He wants me to give in, to turn on the boys I know, love, and trust with my life. A life I hope I get to live…soon.

They have to wonder where I am. Jaz must wonder why I didn't come back out front. I'm sure they found Crystal's body. It's only been a day, though, and they won't expect that I'm a *guest* of the Broken Bows unless someone told them.

I doubt the Bows sent a thank you note or a ransom, so I'll bet they have no idea that I'm in their *care.* Narrowing my gaze at Busta once more before I turn away, I set the cup down with a thankful belly and a more confused heart. I can't figure out what his intentions are. Does he think I'll crack because of a drink? Because he's being kind to me with that shirt?

Being kind would be setting me free.

Setting us *all* free.

CHAPTER 17

Oubliette
Day Three

The floor is fucking cold. The room is giving me a chill in this flimsy shirt, and I'm starting to smell like the rest of the women in here. I finally used that bucket, though I despised every moment of it.

I haven't given up on the women here, even as they've given up on themselves. I hoped that I'd have at least someone to converse with, beyond the small bug I watched crawl through the bars earlier this morning, but still nothing.

They whisper between themselves. A few I've heard speaking in dull tones about me, the white-haired witch. Okay, not witch, but I try to act like I can't understand the Spanish they speak, and that the nasty things they say about me aren't derogatory.

In the cage closest there's a small girl, no more than ten. Jet-black hair, tangled and twisted, oily, and a total mess. Her wide brown eyes are searching and imploring as she looks through the vast area. She's looking for someone, and even though she's in a cage with another young girl around her age, with a woman whom could pass as her mother, she's sullen and devoid of emotion. I tried once to ask her how long she'd been here and if she was alone like me, but she never replied. I gave in yesterday after a few hours of the same. I don't think there's much that could get through to her at this point, and it's unfortunate. They're weak if they've given into their fate and can't find solace in the neighbor that can possibly offer comfort.

Not me. I won't give in, at least not yet. It's only been three days, and I know there's more that can happen. I can still prevail.

Busta traipses down the steps like a herd of elephants, stopping at my door. Each time he's come down—at least three times a day—I've ignored him. I tell myself today will be no different. This is his second trip. He's checking the women, checking that they've eaten the supplied food, and topping off water if necessary. He growls as he cleans the makeshift latrines, but I don't feel sorry for him in the least.

"Wish to give anything up, my queen?"

I don't reply.

"You seem cold. Are you cold, Obi?" he says in a sarcastic tone.

Pressurizing my teeth, I tighten my jaw and seal my lips shut.

"That shiver in your shoulders tells the truth, Obi."

Condescending prick. "I'm not shaking with cold. It's with fury."

He laughs out loud. "You speak! I thought I'd shocked you into silence."

Shit. Fuck. I tried so hard to zip it, and one comment throws me into the fray.

"You're an asshole and I hate you," I spit out.

Placing a heavy hand around a bar near where I sit, he bends down, bringing himself to my level. "I'm not who put you in this position, Obi. You did." In a softer tone, almost pleading, he says, "Just tell me something and I'll let you out. I'll keep to our deal. I'll release someone else." Looking to the cage closest, eyeing the young girl, he raises his chin. "What about her? I think she could do with a shower."

Staying silent, I flare my nostrils and wait him out. I know he'll shut up again and continue on if I ignore him.

With a sidelong look, hoping to seem un-fazed by his attention, I feel his gaze focused my way. "I'm impressed with you, Obi." Reaching out a hand, he strokes my long hair. "I thought you'd break. I thought you'd cry and beg to be released. You're stronger than I gave you credit for." Standing, looking down at me, his serious tone is hard to deny. "But you're stubborn attitude isn't helping anyone else."

That hurt. I hate to admit it, but it's the truth. My attitude *is* what has put me here and stopped me from helping others.

I can't do it, though. I can't give up something I *don't* know. Yeah, I've heard snippets here and there at Humble, but nothing that could be considered viable as intel, even if I wanted to. Which I don't. Death and Jazzy are like family. The Horsemen too. I'd never intentionally hurt Curse, Destroyer, Trigger, or any of the other guys. They have their faults, but they've never been mean to me. They've never been anything but the sweetest people. I know the public persona of being a biker is all bad—evil, dangerous, and dark souls with no redemption—but it's not true of the Horsemen. They're the sweetest. I've seen them do rides for tots, send around a collection jar for a local that needs surgery, and even helped a stripper that was down on payments. They're not like the Bows—they're nice.

Tuning out Busta, he finally walks off. Nearing the other occupants, still attempting to get my goad, he talks as he wanders. "They don't talk to you because they know. They know you have the power to help a few and you're not. So you're just as much the enemy as I am." He continues as he sticks me with his words. "She won't tell you that you're pretty on the outside. You're ugly because you won't help." Pausing at the cage of the little girl, he pops the lock on the only defense she has against him—the heavy door. She scuttles to the far side, hiding in the corner nearest to where I sit, cowering from him. Peering over, realizing where she is, she shifts away as fast as she'd appeared.

"See?" He's so confident and smug. Her move confirmed his comment. "She wants nothing to do with you."

That's it, I'm pissed off. "Stop telling me it's my fault! It's not. It's yours." I smack my foot against the floor. "*You're* the scum of the earth. You and your *brotha's* will be escorted out by police at some point. Your little trafficking business will shut down. I may not see it, but when I read it in the paper I'll be excited, Mr. Tough Biker. I'll be happy that you're dragged away to jail." I've had enough of being nice and sweet. It's getting me nowhere. Being silent only sets barriers that don't matter.

"You know what I see, Busta?"

He smirks before walking farther into the cage of the little girl and her partnered captives.

Appearing at the corner nearest to me, he says, "Go on then. Tell me, Obi."

Fine. "You're the guy with no one to care for, no one to love, and no one who loves you. You've been in the dark so long that you're blind to human decency. You can't see that you and your little business venture is damaging to others. Until it touches you personally, you'll grind on and continue the same." I point to the little girl with the nappy, unkempt hair. "She isn't afraid of me. She's afraid of my strength. She doesn't have the strength to fight you and it scares her. She's afraid to have hope. *I* give her hope." Standing up, I move toward the side where he stands. "You're a broken soul. I see through you, Busta. You've no one to care for because you hurt anyone who came close. Your family left you, or you left them. There's no women close to you because you can't love. These women are seen as products because they're the reminders that you can't love. No one wants you." Blowing out the heavy breath after my evil diatribe, I'm softer as I smile at him. "I feel sorry for you. You can't feel love."

When I finish, I see the deadly gleam in his eyes. He's pissed. His hands are tightly balled and his jaw is set. I've pushed too far. Setting the food down, the bottles of water and stepping out of the cage he doesn't even close the door. With deadly intent, he slowly walks toward me. His feet are silent, the sound from before when he wished to push me is now devoid in each footfall.

Crossing my arms, I wait for the inevitable interaction when Busta stops at the lock of my door. With a singing click, the door releases. Pulling it, he steps inside. His body is rigid, his stance deadly, and his movements are contained.

Coming to a stop at my feet, I look up at him defiantly.

"Oubliette, I'm doing everything in my power to control my temper." His breath is so close—so heated, that I feel it brush my forehead. With a heavy gaze, his voice comes out in a whispered, threatening tone. "You don't know me. You don't know my past or anything about me except what you expect based on the situation, so I'm going to give you a break on your ignorance. Though I will say this, if you *ever* disrespect my family or me again, it will be the last thing you do. No amount of begging or turning intel on the Horsemen will save you." Raising a hand, he places a finger under my chin, lifting my face to look at him directly. "I'm not the sum of what you see. I'm not cold to this, I'm not dead inside. I see it. I *hate it*."

Softly, I tell him, "Then do something."

"I can't." His demeanor changes and his gaze softens. "I can't."

Without thought, I raise a hand. Touching his face purely on instinct, I brush his dark, rough beard as his green glowing eyes pierce me.

"I wish there was a way for us to meet in another time and in another place. I would've taken you on a date. I would've shown you what a real man could be." With his eyes tightening again, he backs up. "But this is how it is."

Clearing his throat and walking to the door, Busta closes it behind him. "Give me what I need and we can stop all this."

With the click, Busta is gone.

CHAPTER 18

Busta

What the ever-loving fuck!

Turning the lock, I felt every tick. I felt like the biggest cock on the planet. I hated it. I despised it, but I had to.

Tromping back up the stairs two at a time, my heart was heavy. I ran straight to the fridge. Pulling out the cooled tequila from the icebox, a cup from the drying rack and filling it halfway, I guzzled two glassfuls before my ass hit the couch.

Yeah, she pissed me off, but the way she softened soothed the demon within, and it turned me on. Wanting to do nothing other than press my hips against hers and show her how much she's affecting me, I've instead gathered my control. Grinding my teeth, I grabbed my spine and locked her ass in the empty cage again.

I had to be the asshole. I had to place her back in there and leave. She's tougher than I thought she'd be. She's not begging for her release, and she's not turning over on the Horsemen.

I'm still amazed. She didn't argue as the lock turned. She didn't bitch, whine, or moan about the cage I'd locked her in after our raging interaction. She stood her ground, arms crossed, scowling. Even now, two days later, she's as quiet as a church mouse.

Fuck, it's hot on her.

Oubliette isn't afraid to go toe-to-toe with me to enforce her opinion, and she's damn near uncrackable.

I pour another half glass of the Tequila I've all but emptied.

"Fucking woman," I mutter to myself, grabbing up the television remote.

I hated that I had to put her in there. Fighting her, I wished nothing more than to kiss those soft lips. I wanted to take her ire and push her attitude to the forefront again. Thing is, if she's that stubborn, there's no way I'm getting any info out of her unless I push her. I'll need to drag her to the edge of her limitations. I'll need her to break…So I do what I have to. If I don't then True has no reason to keep her alive or to let her lose.

Who am I fucking kidding? She's never getting free of us. The only way out is through slavery to a man that will use her as a sex toy until he kills her.

I need her to hate me, even as I hate me for doing it. I have to make her despise everything about this place.

That first day, True called, wondering if she gave anything up, and when I'd told him I thought we needed a few days, he laughed. Then yesterday, he called again and said he would be bringing us a present soon, one that he thought could bend her to our will, or that could be more useful. I doubt it, but good on him for trying.

If I thought offering to help others would be a way to get through to her, and she hasn't cracked seeing the destitute souls, then there's no way that a *present* will loosen her tongue.

Her resolve will bring me to the edge. I'll have to dig deep to be the asshole she expects.

I'll have to believe in it too.

Fuck.

CHAPTER 19

Oubliette

As the days have passed, I've watched intently. I've watched for a chink in his armor, looking for an opening. I hoped for a way out. After our hateful interaction, I was turned on by his seething anger.

I'm a masochist. I want him steamed and ready to attack me. He was unbelievably and undeniably sexy.

Since then, I've watched to see if he's the monster I thought he was. For two days, I've catalogued his moves. With each of the inhabitants, he'd left in their cages packets of food and bottles of water. For the youngest girls, he added a single cookie. Either he has a heart or a mandate to make them feel less damaged. For me, he's left me a protein shake every morning. The first one, before our interaction, I tried my best to ignore it, but seeing how and what he did after the fact, I gave in and accepted his kindness. That, and I was starved.

Each time he came down, he'd ask that same question and act as if he was the hardened asshole once more. "Wish to give up anything, my queen?" he'd say as he passed. When I wouldn't answer, he'd walk away.

Sitting in my corner, I watch as he does the same thing he's done each day. He's regimented in his movements, in his activities, and in the way he's watched me.

Sitting on a stool at the edge, he peers over. His looks at me quizzically, like I surprise him. I think he's amazed I haven't broken. I think he and I, in other circumstances, might have gone on that date he spoke of. His dark, tattooed skin is something I'd love to trace with my fingers. I'd like to see if there are veins of brown or blue within his green eyes. I'd like to see if he has scars on his face under that thick beard. If his smile reacts when I tell a joke, or if he can laugh out loud when he's happy.

The ring of a cell phone breaks the silence, and the look on Busta's face tells me something profound is about to happen here. There's something akin to fear as he takes the call.

CHAPTER 20

Busta

"Yeah." Grabbing up my phone and answering a call from Nock, I rise from my chair at the railing and take a seat on one of the couches. I've worked through the beer supply. The whiskey and Tequila are gone, so is most of the protein shakes, since I've shared them with Oubliette. I could really go for a burger drenched in mayo.

I've watched a rerun marathon session on dinosaurs, the Jurassic stuff, and the making of the animatronics. There's no cable here, and only two channels on the television—news and the dinosaurs. I hate news. It's nothing but grim reminders that *everything* is bad news.

"I have a new addition. I think you'll like this one just as much as the last." As he says it, I hear the mirth in his voice.

"Yeah?" Pushing my slightly stiffening erection to the side again, just from the mere thought of my current guest, my cock comes to life. I've had no way to release the building pressure. I won't use my hand, and I refuse to use someone here. I despise either choice. I'll gladly abstain.

Oubliette ticks all my boxes, even the angsty, stubborn, hate-filled edges of her. I can't imagine taking anyone other than her to my bed. I've always gone for the whores, those that I have no connection to. My past and my current life don't mix. I'd chance discovery. Oubliette, though, she's more important than I'd like to admit. More than my base desires. Not to mention, her tight body, soft curves, hips I could hold for days, and lips that beg to be bitten.

Laughing into the phone, Nock pulls me from my train of thought. "Oh, this one is just as nice, buddy. Just as nice."

No chance.

I know he won't give up until I relent. "Fine. When will you be here?"

"We're swingin' around the block." Nock is way too happy about bringing in this new girl, and he didn't even offer to bring me lunch. "I can't wait to see what she'll fetch," he adds before hanging up.

Nock is a deviant fucker in his tastes, but not in a pedophile kind of way, just dark and twisted. If he thinks she's worth good money, it tells me she's decidedly legal.

Pocketing my phone, I finish off the last of my bottle before laying it on the table, but I don't quite make it. Clinking as it skirts the metal edge on the table, I watch it spin. Rising up and huffing out a deep breath, I start toward the stairs.

I've made a vow that I won't look in her cage, mainly because I don't want to see her disappointment as I walk past her for the door, but also because it could try my personal resolve to leave her there once the new girl shows.

The overriding need to taunt her is almost too hard to pass up, though. I instinctively look, telling myself it's because she could be picking the lock with a fingernail.

Bounding down the stairs, heavier than I need to, I reach the ground floor and pause at her cage. Sitting in the corner, legs tucked up, arms curled around them with her gaze firmly planted on mine, she smiles. "Hi, asshole."

If I ever needed the cookie cutter example of what a resting bitch face looks like, hers would be the picture below. With narrowed eyes, slow fluttering lashes, and a hard, thin set to her lips, she's ready to rip me apart with her words.

Ignoring her barb, because it's the truth, I stop at her door and smile, because I'm a fucking martyr. I want to feel her ire.

"Hello, Obi. Ready to give me something?"

As I pick up the now empty plastic cup I'd given her earlier and smile, she quips, "Keep walking." Leaning against the bars, she inspects her nails. "I have a hangnail more important than you."

"Contrary to belief, my world doesn't re-volve around you, Obi." Calling her by the nick-name she hates, I actually feel blood rise in my cock as I see her visibly twitch. When she doesn't speak further, I continue to walk on, a little more smug than before. I like this war of words. I like her annoyed.

Arriving at the side door, I pull the key from my pocket. Lifting the small electronic fob, I press it to the panel and watch as the blue light switches to red. This building's security is mini-mal, yet hi-tech. The door that Oubliette and I entered through, tracks the clicks in and out. Seeing that Oubliette and I hadn't clicked out, it locked the moment we entered. Without this fob, me and her, along with all the women and girls in here, would perish without some type of intervention. There's no way to bring in food. All the windows are sealed shut, the doors are on system locks, and no one can enter until we un-lock it from this side. It keeps the contents tight-ly tucked away.

Let's say that one of the guys gets a bit too close to a cage with his key, you still can't exit without the code. It's a revolving code that we receive in texts.

Secure.

Contained.

Intelligent.

Entering the current code, 44562, the light switches to purple. Pulling the door open when I hear the knock, Nock enters with a thin, well-dressed woman. The interesting part is the bag over her head.

I snicker. "What's up with her?"

"She kept biting me. I had to gag her." Shoving her forward, he grins. "The cuffs were for fun."

"And the bag?"

"She's a smart one. I didn't want her knowing where we were going. She'd tell her fuckin' brother."

I'll ask on that later. He walks in, forcing her forward. "Where's True?" I ask.

Wrestling the merchandise forward, Nock gives me that grin that says there's trouble brewing. "He had other business."

"Why'd you leave him unprotected?"

"He had to rush home, man. Something about DG." I have a good feeling I know why, but I wait for him to explain further. "He asked for Strike's bow to be brought out of storage."

"Well fuck." Death and spilled blood are sure to follow when Strike picks up a bow. We don't see him much, and I'm pretty content with that.

Fighting with the girl as she tries to knee him again, Nock grabs her by the back of her neck. "Hold the fuck still! Jesus fucking Christ, woman!"

There's not much to her, and he outweighs her by at least a hundred pounds, but she's full of fucking fire. Dressed in thin jeans, a white shirt and pin-like heels, she curses him through the gag, fighting him every step of the way.

"She's definitely a tough one," I joke. Unlocking the door to the cage beside Obi, I help Nock unbolt her hands and keep her still. Making sure the outside door relocks, she swings wildly, trying to hit anything close.

She's a tough little lady, and I admire that.

Once the lock is clicked and we're out of harm's way, she throws off the bag, loosens the knotted cloth from her mouth and squeals, "You sons of bitches! You'll fucking pay for this! You have no idea how much I want to kick your ass! Come back in, you fucking asshole, so I can shove my heel so far down your throat you'll pee sparkles."

Oh yeah, I like this one. I almost want to open the door and let her at Nock.

"Jazzy? What the fuck!"

Oubliette stands and rushes to the newcomer. Their hands barely touch, as the cages are set far enough away from one another that contact isn't possible. It keeps them from finding a way to escape.

"Oh my God! Why are you here?" Turning away, reaching a hand through the bars, Jazzy spins on us. "Why is she here? Why are we here?"

Pocketing his key, Nock smacks me on the shoulder before starting toward the stairs. "I could go for a beer. You in, Busta?"

Without a word, I follow. I make a conscious decision to walk off without looking her way. The response from her will be that of appalled, disgusted, and shocked. Her whole being will break me.

Fuck, I'll crack.

I'll pull them both from the cages and bring them upstairs for drinks.

I'll fuck this up. I'll fuck it all up.

"Why are we here? What is this place?"

With my boots clacking on the stairs, I continue up as Obi calls out, "Busta! Don't turn and ignore us! Answer her, you fucking asshole!"

That's right.

I'm a hardened, soulless man.

I'm an asshole.

She doesn't affect me. I *can't* let her affect me.

I'm calling bullshit…on myself.

CHAPTER 21

Oubliette

I watch Busta and the guy they call Nock retreat up the stairs. I'm in shock. I don't get it. I don't understand the circumstances behind this.

I get why I was taken. I saw something I shouldn't have, and they're hoping I'll roll over on the Horsemen. But Jazzy? Why take her if they have me? Why is she here? And why isn't her brother busting down the door to get her back?

When Busta hangs his head and tucks his tail between his legs, I know he won't turn and release me. Not now. Not while his buddy's here.

Fuming, I take a seat on the floor again, close to where Jazzy's cage is. I need answers.

"What happened?" Jazzy blurts out before I can say a word.

"Fuck, Jaz. I was just about to ask you the same fucking thing. Why are you here?"

With her back against the steel bars and her heels in hand, she tosses one across the space. "Fuck! Oubliette, I have no idea what the hell is going on." Looking up the stairs, she screams out, "You little dick motherfuckers will pay for this! You will, you know! My brother will drag you behind his Harley until there's nothing but bones left!"

She's pissed, and rightly so.

Jazzy sits down. "I'm afraid to touch one fucking thing in here."

Looking around the space, seeing what I've already seen, she stares into the faces of the destitute and damaged women that can do nothing but stare back. "What the hell is this place?" she finally asks.

"It seems the Broken Bows are human traffickers. Surprise!" I try to sound lighthearted and cynical, but in all honesty, I'm disgusted.

"Traffickers? Fuck! I hope to hell my brother and his boys have nothing to do with this." She grinds her teeth growls out, "If they do, I'll castrate every single one of them."

And I know she will. Jazzy doesn't take shit. Not from her brother, not from the club, not from me, and especially not from someone she doesn't know. I'll bet she took a chunk out of that guy Nock when she bit him.

"Give it to me, Oubliette."

Running down the circumstances of my situation, from the death of Crystal to my recent incarceration, I watch her take it all in. She's not processing it like she wants all the details and needs to know how to console me. Nope, not Jazzy. She's cataloging their demise. Where the knife will sink in, how their deaths will be, and how badly she wants to display their genitals in a vase like flowers, which is something I'd assist with in my hatred for them.

I've detailed their deaths a few times now myself. It'll be joyous.

When I'm done, I ask what happened to her.

"Well, it seems that Trigger came looking for you when Radish turned tail down the hall. Finding her scratching at the door to the alley, he found Crystal, but no you after he searched. Immediately, we closed the club and went into lockdown. I stayed at the club while we arranged for each of the girls to get to the compound or home, and while that happened, I stayed behind waiting on a ride. Anyway, I was alone, hanging at the club when *that* ugly bastard walked in. Sweet as pie and smiling like a Cheshire cat, he waltzed right into the bar. I told him we were closed and continued on with my cleaning, not giving him another thought.

"But the bastard didn't leave. He just stood there grinning, looking all smug. We had a few choice words. He pulled a gun and told me if I wanted to see the sun through my eyes instead of the back of my head, I needed to be his date. So here I am. After almost a week of shifting from car to car in a trunk, and a dingy apartment strapped to a radiator, I'm in a shithole that makes shitholes look good." Shifting, trying to find a comfortable position, Jazzy pauses for dramatics. Looking back at the jerks upstairs, she yells out, "Fuck, this floor is uncomfortable! Come down here so I can gouge out your eyes!"

"Won't do you any good, Jaz." I gaze up at them as they clink their beers together. "They're just like the rest—conditioned to be good soldiers. It's club business, we know the drill."

"Yep." pointing two fingers in salute to the pair upstairs, "Fuck you both! Lemmings!"

Jazzy has never towed the club line to perfection. She kind of cuts the string, creates her own path, and causes mayhem where she goes. Of which makes for entertaining conversations in the club. Death—or Bennett to Jazzy—is a second generation in the Four Horsemen. Bennett and Jasmine's dad, Discord, started the club after Vietnam. It's profitable. With their dealings in porn, strip clubs, bike shops and Humble, they're on the up-and-up. Sure, they deal in darker stuff, but I don't think they're truly dangerous like the Broken Bows seem to be.

Why is that? Why would the Bows have any care for a clean club like the Horsemen?

"Jaz, gotta ask you something." I lean as comfortably as I can on the bars.

"Yeah. Go."

"This is bothering me. If the Horsemen are on the up-and-up, why do the Bows want intel on them? Why take me? Why take you?"

She starts to giggle hysterically, finding what I asked funny.

Gathering her composure, she turns to me and clears her throat. "Sorry. That was fucking funny, O."

"What the hell was funny?" I'm thoroughly confused.

"Oubliette, they're not on the 'up-and-up'. The Four Horsemen are nowhere even remotely on the right side of the law. They're the largest supplier of drugs in Corona and surrounding areas. Not to mention, the chop shops and whores. They're *far* from clean, sister."

"So I've been working for the better part of six years in a biker owned club that I thought were the not so bad guys, when in actuality, they've been just as bad as these jackasses?" I toss my arms up in defeat. Not at the Horsemen or Jazzy, or even the cocksuckers upstairs. Nope. I'm annoyed that I was that fucking naive.

"Just fucking great. Now I get why he thought I had tons of intel. I'm a bartender in a gentlemen's club that deals in drugs and hookers."

"Intel? They want intel on the boys through you?" She rolls her eyes. "Jesus. I'm so sorry, babe."

"What do you have to be sorry for? That I was stupid and blind to everything, or that I'm worth nothing to them once they find out?"

Slouching back against the bars, Jazzy tilts her head skyward. "Yeah, that. Those dogs were barking at the wrong girl."

CHAPTER 22

Busta

"So she's Death's baby sister?"

Nock bends down to rummage through the fridge. "That's right."

I can only imagine the grin on his face. Nock is a deviant fucker. He likes discord and strife. He's the one that if you're out for blood, make sure he's at the front. He's as messy as you can get. I'm not a saint by any expression of the word, but he puts me to shame with his ideals. I never would've thought to use an exhaust pipe that way before.

I digress.

I once watched him make his way through a tweaker building, and with a silencer and a bow, he took everyone out, one by one. That gun made a mess, and the bow made an impression. He has the road name of Nock from how fast he can load a bolt into a bow and shoot with amazing accuracy. He's meticulous, calculating, precise in his aim, and he's careful to leave the only message that they'll understand. The Broken Bows are not to be fucked with.

On a ride, he's the best man to have with you. On a hit, he's the one you want at your side.

Tossing me a brew before uncapping his own, he starts talking about Jasmine. "Yeah, she's my kinda girl. Single. Sexy as fuck and nasty to boot. I think I'm in love."

Fucker's kinda joking, but it's the truth. For him, there's nothing better. Someone who can give it back to him tenfold is his match made in hell. He's not a roses and fucking flowers kind of guy. He's a tied to the bed, screaming, blood from his knife work, and that sinister fucking grin of his if she's still fighting.

Guzzling his beer, clearing out at least half of the contents in one swig, Nock turns to the edge of the balcony. "Look at this, Busta."

Grabbing up my beer, I stand beside him.

"See them? See those poor restless and beaten souls?" Hanging his bottle over the edge, he leans on his elbows, staring into the sea of cages.

"Of course I do." I lean my arms on the railing next to him, waiting on Nock's grand epiphany.

"This is what I see. Twenty thousand, ten thousand, five thousand, and a hundred grand. I see dollar signs, nothing more. Their whole value is contained in the sum of their cunts, lips, and ability to shut the fuck up. If they can suck cock and take it in the ass like a champ, they're worth more if their lips stay glued together. If they can't, I don't care either. They were bought and paid for, which makes them none of my business anymore." This I know. I hate it. I despise it. But I get it.

"Why the education, Nock?"

"Because they weren't about to let us continue our business through Corona to the docks. We had to show them who's boss. They were wrecking our transport and our warehousing. True had to give them a reason." He points below. "She's the reason. Well, I guess both of them, but that skinny, big-mouthed one will change the power for us. Get me?"

"Yeah, man. I get ya." She's bait, leverage, and damage control, all wrapped up in a neat fucking package.

Taking a swill of my brew, I venture a look at the two women. The newcomer hasn't quit fucking yelling at Nock, and I don't damn well blame her.

"You should be careful. I'd hate to laugh as you fall to your death!" she yells up.

"So what's the deal with the other one?" I ask. I've yet to get the full story on why Obi's here. I'm fuckin' interested.

Nock swigs another mouthful, then tosses the bottle. Smashing it everywhere below, it rains glass into the enclosures. Without remorse, he asks, "Interested?"

Leaning on the railing, stroking my beard and stretching my shoulders, I school my features. As I drink down the last of my own beer and set it on the table beside me, I answer, trying to sound aloof. I won't let him know I'm interested. "Nah."

"The blonde saw something she shouldn't have. At least, that's what True told me," Nock divulges. Walking away from the rail and reaching into his bag, Nock grabs up his cigarettes. Pulling one from the case, offering the pack to me, I wave him off. Lighting one up, pocketing the crinkly package in his jeans, he blows smoke rings into the vacant air. "You know what it was?"

He takes another drag off his cigarette. "Yeah. True killed Crystal at Humble." Pointing below, he flicks the dead embers off his cig. "She saw it."

I was always surprised that Crystal survived as long as she had in the lifestyle of the Bows.

Two years younger than the twins, Crystal was raised in the life. Her pale skin in a club run, owned and created by brothers, her difference caused her to be the outsider. The anomaly.

I personally liked Crystal. She was sweet. She didn't deserve the crass torment she was subjected to because of the color of her skin. No matter what, she was True's sister. If he killed her, I doubt he'll let that be known to anyone else but myself and Nock. Nock, because the two of them are closer than brothers. Nock'll defend and follow blindly behind True in all decisions. Myself, I'm not so happy with that, now knowing that taking Oubliette was to keep her quiet. I also know that if any of the brother's find out, there's no way True will gain the seat as Pres.

Fuck. I get it now.

Looking below at the sweet face of Obi, I see that I'm looking at a woman who will either die or wish she had. He gave me a project that was destined to fail.

I was interested in Oubliette and why True thought she was important. Now, the more I listen to Nock, the more I realize how she became tangled up in something that's bigger than her.

This won't go well for her.

That cage may be her new address until shipment day. The only thing that could save her could cause my death. If I help her escape, we could both die.

Shit.

CHAPTER 23

Oubliette

Picking glass out of my caged area, I set it outside the confines, and Jazzy does the same. Fucking prick who tossed that down...I swear, I'll find a way to slit his throat with it.

Sitting in the corner, talking to Jazzy, the two of us plot quietly. Yeah, if either Busta or Nock come close, they'll find out how crazy we can be. We're not like the others in here. *They've* given in. They've decided their destiny is no longer theirs. Not me. Not Jaz. We're getting out of here. If I have to use my body, fine. If I have to act sultry when I'd rather gag, then sure. I'm not resigning myself to a life of servitude to *any* man who thinks he owns me.

I own me.

I live for me.

Venturing a gaze up at the two of them hanging out on the balcony, I look for a weakness in their armor. A chink. That's when Busta peers at me with sadness in his eyes. His eyes give everything away when his face doesn't speak at all. The lack of laugh lines tells me he's a consummate actor. He was *chivalrous* by not interrupting me as I slept in that bedroom. He told me to close my eyes before he turned on the lights. Yeah, he put me in here, but when Nock arrived, I could see the disappointment. He'd expected to remove me from here after he'd taught me a lesson. With Jazzy arriving, his opportunity had been removed.

Nock is a wild card. Looking at him, I see only malice and sadistic tendencies. He acts like life is carefree and fun, but he's a twisted mess.

He *tossed* a beer bottle at us!

He knew it would break and he didn't care. Even now, I hear him loudly express his intentions with our bodies.

"Brother, if she wasn't Death's sister, I'd already have had my turn with every one of her holes. That tight body would've broke." Licking his lips, he glares down at Jazzy. It's disgusting. "I wanna hear her cry. And the other one, I'll leave her to you if you want a run at her."

Busta's eyes never leave mine, but they tell the truth as his mouth spouts lies. "Who says I didn't already have her?"

Bumping Busta's shoulder, he laughs sickly. "I've seen you in action, brother. That woman should be in tears. There's no way you broke her. I think I might, though, seeing you've left her intact." Smacking his hands together, he starts toward the stairs.

Keeping my eyes locked on Busta, I don't acknowledge Nock as he bounds down the stairs. Busta's eyes are expressive, even without a flick in his facial expressions. The twinkle in the edges show fire. Eventually, turning my head away, I look straight at Jazzy. In her cage, she's inspecting her nails, acting totally disinterested in his supposed threat to our bodies. I shrug and she smirks. We're not afraid. He gave us ammunition against his threat. Palming the small piece of the bottle bottom that I kept, I feel the edge of it as it rests in my hand. Her piece is out of view, but I know it's beside her, ready for the attack.

I'll cut the fuck out of my hand, but his neck will leak. I'm not going down without a fight.

Pausing at my door, I hear him using his fob to release the cage. "Hell, she's not a skinny bitch." Grasping his belt, he tosses it out of the cage. Releasing the jean button, he pulls it, then tears down his zipper slowly. Reaching within, Nock palms his cock, sneering in such a way that I can't see anything but his sick intentions, even as I try to ignore him.

Come on. I'm ready for you, you sick fuck.

Holding the glass so tight that the blood trickles down my palm, I rest it out of sight below my leg. Nock is so invested in his opportunity to have his way with me, that he's making errors in judgement.

He tosses his gun into the vacant area behind the cage. He's expecting a weak woman, but how easily he forgets where they found us. We're not meek mice.

"Sweet. I'll bet there's not a scar on her. That'll change in a moment, darlin'." Turning to Jazzy, he smacks the bars, rattling the cage she inhabits. The other women and girls that surround us visibly cower. They've been this way for far too long to even consider fighting. I haven't eaten properly in days, but I still have enough fight in me to take him down.

"Come here, cunt," he says to me. "Let me show you what a real man can do." As he moves closer, I slowly look up. Looking him in the eyes, I see the madness of his dark heart. "Oh, you'll be so fun to break." He glances over at Jazzy once more as he stands directly in front of me, smiling at her. "Watch. Learn what I like."

Ignoring the barbs, I ready for an attack.

Watching his pants fall low—intentionally done to cause fear, he bends low at the hips, crouching only inches from my face. With his hand, he raises my chin to meet his hardened and deadly stare. Just the opening I needed.

"Sweetie, this'll be—"

Swiping the glass quickly across his throat, his voice becomes a gargled noise. I've dealt a blow that was meant to cause maximum damage.

I *won't* be someone's toy.

I won't be a pawn in any game.

With deadly strength, he grasps my neck tightly, adding as much pressure as possible while he comes to grips with the death that's swiftly taking him. His blood spills across my clothing, and I can see how cleanly it sliced.

His hands remain tight around my neck, but if I take this twisted man with me, there'll be one less prick in the world. I can't help all the women and children here, but at least they may see there's still something worth fighting for. I'm not ready to die, though. I'll fight to live.

As stars cloud my vision, with air barely flowing into my lungs, I drop the glass and claw at his hands. I can hear Busta rushing down the stairs as Nock's strength wanes. Pulling at his fingers, frantically peeling the tips away, I try to back away. I watch as the mirth that once lit those dark brown eyes becomes that of fear and understanding. I shouldn't, but I relish his demise.

I *should* feel bad that I ended someone's life.

I *should* feel that his death was unnecessary. Right?

I don't.

It was his death or mine.

Finally releasing the last of his grip on my throat, I push away. Receding into the opposing corner, crouching and looking to Jazzy, I cough out the pain. Every breath is labored and strained.

It aches. But at least I'm alive to feel it.

The same thing can't be said for the man bleeding out a river of red.

As I see Busta approaching, I pick up the shard once more.

CHAPTER 24

Busta

"Jesus. Fucking. Christ!"

Watching the train wreck in slow motion bounding down the stairs, barely touching even one, I cleared the space in short time. Coming to a sliding stop within the cage, I bend down over Nock's body and flip him over.

"Fuck, Nock! Fuck you! You cocky son of a bitch. Thinking you could…Fuck!"

What a dumb move. He didn't think before hopping into the cage with her.

I *know* what he was thinking. He thought she was just another weak woman he could best, control, dominate and break. He was wrong. Obi and Jazzy aren't those poor fucking souls ready for sale.

The dumbass forgot he gave her the weapon. Smashing that bottle above their cages, he gave them their ammunition.

Trying to cover the wound, I attempt to staunch the flow, the blood freely streaming between my fingers. I know that his end is close. Thick and pumping, his life is escaping. I can't do a damn thing to stop it.

As realization dawns in Nock's eyes. I can't believe that I'm watching him die. He's by no means one of my favorites, but he's not the worst by any stretch of the imagination either.

"I can't help, man. There's nothing I can do." His eyes say the same.

Holding his hand, gripping it tightly as the final moments arrive—when the last rider takes him, I sit until I'm holding his slack hand.

Sitting back on my haunches, I take in the disaster. I'm coated in his blood. His eyes cloud over as he finally takes his final breath. His death will be a *big* fucking problem. I see the circumstances changing drastically, not only for the captured, but for the captor too.

Coughing, straining to gather her breath, I look to Oubliette as she breaks the silence. Still gripping the bottle shard tightly, she points it my way as she tries hard to gulp down air.

"Do you understand what you've done?" I ask Obi.

Looking away from Nock's slackened body, with death only in his features, I hold her gaze. Straining to speak, she pulls in air, then coughs. Rising, I move to approach her, but change my mind. She holds the chip of glass toward me, and I can tell she's not only frightened I'll cause her harm, but that I'll kill her for what she's done.

"You can't hurt me with that," I tell her.

"I…hurt…him," Obi states, before coughing deep once more.

Gripping my gun, I pull it from my waist-band and bring it forward. "I have a gun. He was stupid enough to underestimate you, but I'm not, Obi." I stand over her. "I'm not about to hurt you. You need help, Obi."

"Fuck…you," she coughs, swinging her makeshift weapon wildly. With great difficulty, she's trying to stay upright and conscious.

She needs a doctor.

"Obi, if it makes you feel better, I could empty this and toss it away, but it won't fix anything if you don't toss the glass away. Let me look at you."

"No!"

"Fine." I won't force her. I'll just wait. It's not going to be long before she passes out from lack of oxygen anyway.

I have all the patience in the world.

Walking out of the cage, closing the door behind me, I leave her locked in with Nock's dead body and start for the stairs. I hate that I'm leaving her once more.

No matter what, I can't break.

I can't toss all this away over a woman.

It's never been a choice, and I don't intend to make it one now.

But seeing the pain in her eyes, I'm really considering it. I can't put my finger on it, but something about Oubliette causes me to doubt that the path I'm on is right.

CHAPTER 25

Oubliette

Watching his retreating form, Busta locks
the door to the cage and heads for the stairs. It
takes all the power I have to stay alert. I won't
show him fear. I won't ask for his help, and I
won't accept it when it's offered.

It's faked. I know it is. Busta doesn't give a
shit about me. I'm the property of his fucking
club until I'm no longer useful.

When it was only me, I knew Busta had a
reason to keep me safe. I had an opportunity to
give him false info that could gain the freedom
for a few poor souls. I figured after a bit of trust I
could get close, and that I could get him loose
enough to gain *my* freedom. With Jazzy arriving—a lifer in the Four Horsemen club—the
daughter of the ex-president and the sister to
the current one, I'm worth less than a tank of
fuel.

"Oubliette, oh my God, girl," Jazzy whispers
in mock shock. "I can't believe you did that!
You're one bad ass bitch." She laughs. "And to
think, Death thought you were too sweet for
him."

What? You've gotta be kidding me? That's the first thing that goes through her head, that her brother thought I was a pushover and too weak for him? I'd love to tell her to go eat a dick, but my willpower is all used up trying to stay alert. Staying awake is a fight.

I begin to cough and can't stop. My throat aches, my head's screaming, and my body's rebelling against the lack of oxygen. Now that Busta's upstairs once more, I release the glass and inspect my hand. The deep gouge courses from my pinky, traversing my palm, then runs all the way down to my thumb. The blood slowly trickles down my wrist as I hang my hand. My adrenaline must be at an all-time high because I don't feel it.

Gripping the edge of my shirt, I tear at the seam until it rips and peel off a section. It takes a ton of effort, but once it's wrapped around my hand, it should slow it. Thing is, now I feel the sting of the cut.

"Oubliette. Sweetie, are you okay? Sorry if I seemed heartless, but I'm in shock you did that. I never thought you had it in you." As I cough a few more times, she grimaces. "You sound awful, love."

I feel awful.

Every breath is painful. Every word I squeak out feels like razors slicing through my chest and throat, and as my body relaxes against the lack of air, I'm slowly passing out.

"Sleep. I'll watch out for you." I hear her say the words, but I hardly comprehend them. As each are spoken, they become garbled.

Laying my head against the bars and closing my eyes, the last thing I see Nock's blood leaching its way toward my feet.

CHAPTER 26

<u>Oubliette</u>

There I was, a princess cut diamond on my finger and a simple white gown. No embellishments, just closer to a slip dress than anything else, and the dark dreamy voice beside me that said, 'I can't wait to yank that dress off. My mouth waters just thinking about it, Obi.'

I can't argue with that logic. 'Why wait for later? Let's leave now.'

'You know why.' Whispering in my ear, he nips my lobe. 'Once we're gone, my tongue will lick you dry. I want you screaming my name all night long.'

Me too. I want that so badly.

Looking around the room, it's apparent that everyone is enjoying themselves. Even though I can't see their faces, I hear their mirth and joy. Each person is dressed up and wearing sick horror faces you would wear to a masquerade ball. Each a different character—Jason, Pinhead, Mike Myers, creepy clowns, Chucky, sadistic rabbits with blood at their teeth, Cujo, and macabre skulls.

Bumping me on the shoulder, I hear a cheerful voice say, 'Isn't this the best wedding reception ever?' I recognize the voice as Jazzy, but her face is all wrong. With a mix of blood, skewed eyes and missing teeth, she's a scary Picasso painting.

Shocked and scared, I pull my hand free of the man I was standing with and back away from Jazzy.

'I need out of here. This isn't right. I can't be here.' I feel their pain, their sadness at my willingness to run away. I should be happy to be in their macabre company, but I'm not.

As I leave the room full of masks, they follow me in concert. The whole thing creeps me out further.

'Oubliette, you can't leave here,' they say.

'You belong here,' they yell out as I run from the room.

'No one wants you like we do.'

'Yes. Like us.'

Tearing off as fast as I can, like Cinderella at the ball, even as I lose a shoe and continue to run, I don't dare acknowledge their calls. I don't look at those surrounding me. I can't handle it.

Tearing away the fear, pulling away from it all, I run until the door is in sight.

I see freedom.

I see light.

I see…my father.

He's tall and proud, dressed in his favorite sweater and jeans.

He looks…great.

But dead men don't look great.

'Obi?' he calls out sweetly.

Moving with swift intent, I race until my arms surrounds his waist. I smell his freshly applied aftershave.

I loved his aftershave.

Even after all this time, when I smell it on someone, I fall apart a little inside. The memory of him always crushes me.

'Daddy?'

'Why are you here, Obi?' he asks.

'I don't know. Please take me home,' I squeak into the tightness of his chest.

'I can't, Sweet Pea.' Pulling back slightly, I plead with him. I'm showcasing my best asset, as he never could deny me when I'd give him the hangdog eyes.

He smiles. 'No one but you could get into a mess such as this, Obi.'

'I want to leave, though. Please. Please take me home.' Pulling back, I take in my father—in all his beauty he morphs. He changes into something dark and unknown. He smiles, but it's not as I remember. It's sinister. It's dark. It's deathly.

'This is your fight, Sweet Pea. Fix it your-self.' His voice is harsh and frightening.

There's no compassion in his tone, no light in his gaze. No fire or love.

'Daddy. Daddy, please.' Even though I'm scared of him, I know he won't harm me. He told me he'd love me to the ends of the earth. Shaking his head quickly, the vision of him changes again. No longer does he have bright blue eyes—they're dark pools. No longer sweet, plump, loving cheeks, but instead, they have a hollow, gray skinned appeal. The effect is cold and an unfettered hatred. Pushing away, moving into the shadows, he creeps out of sight, leaving only bright red where his eyes once glowed ee-rily. 'Wake up, Obi,' he says.

Taking a step closer, I yell, 'No! I want to go with you!'

"Wake up, Obi!" I hear Jazzy shout with force.

Opening my eyes with a start, I immediately regret it. Lying on the floor, staring into the blank eyes of Carter, I scramble back, yelling at the top of my lungs.

No sound escapes.

My throat aches, my lungs sear, and my head screams. I'm freaking out as I stare into his deadened eyes. The whole situation of my capture has gone from super fucked up to Armageddon in under a day.

I murdered a biker!

I murdered someone in cold blood. Someone who lies mere feet from me.

Clawing at the bars, I try to move as far away as I can, but there's nowhere to run. There's nowhere to hide that his death won't haunt me.

"Obi!" Jazzy yells again, even as I concentrate all my attention on the dead guy. "Oubliette, look here. Don't look at him. Look at me, sweetie. Look. At. Me."

Tearing my eyes from his hollow ones, I venture a peek at Jazzy.

"That's it, honey. Keep looking at me. It's just us here."

My breathing is shallow and short. Anything more and my throat burns. That, and my hand hurts like a motherfucker. With a fresh bandage, one I didn't place on it, stings from the pain. It feels tight, like it's been stitched.

As I move to speak, Jazzy holds up a hand. "Don't. Just don't. I can see the pain in your eyes." Resting against the bars, she reaches out toward me. "Busta came down and stitched up your hand last night. It'll hurt for a while, and speaking will be difficult too. That large ring around your throat must feel pretty raw."

Touching it out of interest, every square inch is sore. Wincing at particularly difficult parts, tears well in my eyes. I think I'm lucky to be alive. If I rest my voice, hopefully things will be okay. Though if I have to stay in a cage with a dead man much longer, I might lose my shit. Sanitary is one thing, *sanity* will be a crushing blow. I'll go insane having his corpse beside me day in and day out until they trade me out.

Pointing to him with a frustrated look on my face, I swing my hands around wildly, hoping it conveys what I mean.

What the fuck!

What the hell do I do about this?

Like, really?

I point upstairs to Busta, who must be cushy and cozy. I can't believe he left me here in these conditions.

Jazzy obviously gains the gist of my word-less conversation, and snapping her fingers to garner my attention, she says, "He's not here. He went out about an hour ago."

I curse internally. Throwing my arms up in my best '*Are you fucking kidding me?*' motion, Jazzy laughs.

It's so frustrating, not being able to convey things in words. I sigh, but it stings. Fuck, everything about me hurts.

"He's been sitting here for the past two nights." She indicates the chair beside my cage. "He left after a call."

I'm confused. I've been out for two whole nights? How am I not dead? I should be starved and dehydrated.

"I only heard a bit of it, but from what I gathered, there's something big going on at their club." Leaning on the bars, she whispers, "We don't have a new handler, but the cameras watch everything—he told me that. I don't know where he was going, but it was after a lengthy conversation with someone who he argued with quite decidedly."

As I pace the clean section of the cell, careful not to look at or step on Carter, she continues. "He was genuinely concerned for you."

Pointing to Carter, I shake my head harshly. If he cared, he would've removed the rotting corpse!

Standing quickly and reefing on the bars, hoping they'll give, I seriously question myself. I'm not a fucking superhero. That shit ain't about to move with my willpower either.

I roll my eyes, not believing her at all.

"Seriously." Standing up and brushing down the dirt from her clothes, Jazzy grins. "He's questioning me for two nights, but not about the club, about you."

Yeah, I seriously have a hard time understanding why I'd be that interesting. Snickering, I groan at the scratch in my throat.

"Careful, love. Quiet. No use in hurting yourself."

Fine. While we're on the subject of quiet, why're the other captives quiet while the jailers are gone?

Turning, I look to the cages of the previously scared souls.

I'm dumbfounded.

Floored.

I'm amazed!

How in the hell did I sleep through all the cages being emptied out?

I motion to the vast, empty containers.

"Obi, you slept through Busta escorting them out. One cage at a time, twelve hours of it. He'd get a text, rise, pull out the inhabitants, then walk them out in handcuffs and blindfolds." She hangs her head. I know Jazzy. She must have asked what was going on. She's forward enough to have been busting his balls on every trip. We know they've been sold off to the sickest bidders, and her opinion would've been loud.

Turning away from her, I vomit in the corner at the thought of what those woman and girls must be going through. I hardly ate anything since before my shift at Humble, and that night, I only had a small plate of fries because of the train wreck Crystal…

Shit!

This all started in blood.

This whole experience has been over someone else's death that I either caused, viewed, or created. Yeah, throwing up hurts my throat that much more, but thankfully, with nothing in my stomach, it's not as bad as it could've been.

Wiping the edge of my mouth and turning from Carter, I hold what composure I have left. Taking a seat on the floor, farthest from him, I curl my head in my hands and consider it all. There's so much pain, destruction, and death. It's overwhelming. When sleeping, the dream may have seemed like something from a movie, but at least the dress was spectacular. At least the voice of the man was soothing and enticing. There were benefits to smelling my father's aftershave.

I thought of all the times that I'd ridden on his shoulders at the county fair, or when we'd lay on the grass at a concert with my brother Grady and our mom. Those times were simple. I felt loved. I felt a part of something good. Since my parents' car wreck years ago, I've had less of those moments. Being Jazzy's friend. That's good. Being a part of the club—not so much. I'm starting to wonder about my career choice too. Maybe I should've worked at a bio-chem. I could've helped with working on a cure for cancer.

What I could do with those skills. Right now, I'm not helping humanity.

If I get out of here, I'm rethinking my lifestyle paradigm.

Oh my God! What Grady must be thinking! He hasn't heard from me in days. My brother must be worried sick.

Grady and I talk almost every day, sometimes more. He tells me about the guys in his firm that want to date me, I tell him no, then he tries to coerce me into a double date with him and his girl Cammi. Cammi—the stuck up prude princess that would have already asked for her death in this situation. She couldn't handle a hangnail, never mind being kidnapped and slammed in a cage. I'm stronger than her at least. Sure, I think she's the wrong girl for my brother, but hell, she's the wrong girl for most guys I know. That's beside the point. Grady has to be losing his shit that I'm not calling or answering him. I bet he's been to my condo to check in on me at least ten times already.

There's another worry to heap on.

I'm just stacking and racking the blame.

Might as well keep it coming, Universe.

That's when the door beeps and our captor returns.

CHAPTER 27

Busta

Plunking my ass in a chair, I looked below at Obi, Jazzy, and the now deceased Nock. For hours, I considered the consequences of his death. True would be losing his shit over it if he didn't have enough problems of his own.

Getting a call from Munch not twenty minutes earlier, I've been contemplating how this will change us as a club.

"We've got issues. DG is dead."

What the ever-loving fuck!

"You're shittin' me." Not like I can take on more problems.

"Yeah, I'm not kidding, man. It's fucked. True's gone off the rails. He even had us take DG to Strike."

"Give me the rundown," I say.

Munch explains that DG went on a run with two of the older members, cussing and going on about how the young ones were too pussy to do what needed to be done. Going out with Victory and Retribution, they took Munch along.

Deciding that there needed to be a face-to-face, that he had to personally control it, DG took three bullets to the chest. Yeah, he took two of the Heartless Bastards with him to hell, but he and Victory took critical damages. DG didn't make it. Victory will be lucky to survive the night, and Retribution is drinking himself into a stupor.

I've been a part of the club for five years now, and over that time, I've both hated and appreciated the leadership of DG. It wasn't how I would've run the club, but I'm not the leader. I knew coming in that the Broken Bows were this way. I didn't have an issue with it, as I had bigger issues. DG would go off on his own rules without asking church, and this was just another example of that. His son True toes the same line.

As Munch finishes, even running down what happened at the parish with Strike, I'm not surprised. DG's dead, True's president now, and his attack has caused a bigger rift with the other clubs.

"Thanks, Munch." Holding my head in my still blood-stained hands, I blow out a heavy breath.

"True wants you to move the product before we end up under attack there. That's a large shipment to lose. When you're done there, come back for church."

"Got it." I don't have another option, I have to do it. The transport company has been called and I'm to package up the wasted souls for their new owners.

Hanging up the line, I set my phone in my lap. This shit is fucked.

War has come to our door and I have no way out. Not in the sense that will save my ass or theirs. With Nock's death, the girls and I are all in this together. The list that Munch sent over stipulated that Obi and Jazzy are expected on the second truck.

I can't do it.

Staring at Obi below, and Nock's congealed blood flowing toward her, I wait for her to pass out so I can help her. I don't trust Jazzy not to try and kill me if I give her the chance while trying to help Obi, so it's up to me. Fixing up her wounds is the least of my problems, though. How will I save her from being sold?

Grabbing my phone, I flip through my contacts, and pause on a name I've not thought of or spoken aloud in years.

King.

It's been five years. Five years of me deep in the thick of it. Five without contact. Five of me doing the job they tasked me with. I've hated that it's been in the background of my mind all along, but it could be a blessing for this cavernous building of corpses. Maybe this one time, I can do something good with the opportunity now presented to me.

Looking at the picture of a whore's legs spread wide open, with the name Trixie, a girl I've been known to fuck, I tap the call button.

"What the fuck are you calling for?" I couldn't have a picture of him or his name as a contact, and Trixie came with a purpose.

Straight to it as always, I shake off his attitude.

"I need an out."

"Why now, Lucius?" Fucking King can be such an asshole. He laces all his conversations with undertones that express his displeasure with your apparent failure. I've seen it firsthand, and I did my best to stay on the outside of it. When I was young, he owned me. No one is more condescending, controlling, or manipulative than Marcus King. I'm more asshole and less of a sorrowful kid than I was back then, but he has the contacts that can make this happen quick.

"I need your help moving a shipment."

"The shit you say? You don't decide, the game does. You're not done playing your part for me, Lucius." For a moment, the line goes quiet. I know better than to interrupt him when he pauses, so I wait. "What do you need?"

I think about it. Can I fix this? Can I correct this without his help? No.

"Transports."

With the line quieting once more, I continue to watch below. I know what I'm doing is right. This is when *we* should intervene. The issues with the club's infighting will mask their release. I can get her out undetected.

"Done." The line goes dead. King's done with me.

Pocketing my phone, I release another heavy sigh. I hope I've done right by them, right by my family, and right by the Bows. They've become my family after all these years. The family I once had is gone, and this intervention won't harm the Bows directly.

I have to help Oubliette and her friend. It's the right thing to do.

Staring at the women below, I *feel* it in my gut.

I've watched, and probably cared more for her well-being than I ever have with anyone before. She's made me question everything. Watching her over these past few days, Oubliette has made me rethink my part in this. In everything.

In everything I do.
Everything the Broken Bows do.

CHAPTER 28

Busta

Now that all the merchandise has been settled, only myself, Death's sister, Oubliette, and the deceased are left. I say the deceased, as there were a few I'd found in the cages too. Carter's need to toss down that bottle offered up a way out for women who felt there was no other way. I can't blame them; I would too.

With no end in sight, would you choose otherwise? Not a fucking chance. I would take the out offered without question. Sometimes the truth hurts, but it's the truth. Death is sometimes the only clear choice.

Escorting them out took time. There were over ninety women and girls in here. I had to keep up the facade that they were taken out for the soul purpose of being slaves.

Secrecy had to be optimal.

After hours of it, I'm fucking tired, and I'm sure it shows.

Walking over to the last two cages, Obi's and Jasmine's, I decide to start with Jasmine first. The contempt in her eyes burns brightly. Good. I want her ire. I don't want her to think I'm the good guy. For this to work, it has to be authentic. She has to be pissed and arguing for her release. She has to want to fight for her life.

Time to be the asshole, Busta. Time to be hated even more.

Stepping up to her cage, I growl, "Come on. Time to go."

Sneering, she turns her head away. "Fuck off. I'm not leaving her here alone with you."

Walking closer to where she sits, I grip her arm through the bars. "You don't get a fucking choice. Get up."

Swiftly, she swings her hand outward through the bars and smiles. "Fuck off."

She'd hidden a piece of that broken glass too. Good. I can't come out of this unscathed. Taking a slow gaze at the cut across my bicep, I smile. "Do I look as stupid as him? Dumb shit underestimated both of you. I don't, Jasmine."

Pulling out my gun and pointing it at her, she grins. "Oh, I fucking dare you, ya pussy. My brother will have your balls for a light afternoon snack after I tell him what you've done. You fucking cunt wrangler."

Now that's a new one.

Chambering a round, I point my gun at Oubliette. "Get the fuck up, now." I see the wheels turn as she contemplates if I'd really hurt either of them. "Drop the glass, bitch."

Listening as it clinks to the floor, I smile internally. I'm winning small victories.

Tucking my gun away from her, I cuff her hands on the safe side of the bars, knowing better than to stand close enough that she can hit me with an outstretched leg. She'll kick me in the balls, and this will be all for nothing.

"Don't make me gag you," I tell her.

Once her hands are cuffed, I shift to Oubliette. At least I have less fear of her acting out. She's locked in a fear far more dangerous than any shard of glass could do. Unlocking her cage, she doesn't even flinch as I step inside. Moving to her, seeing the disarray, the blood seeping across the floor and the puke in the corner, I know this needs to happen now. This needs to be shut down.

Walking the short distance to her tiny frame, I bend low and speak to her softly. I don't wish to startle her. "Oubliette, it's time to go." Raising her chin to bring her eyes up to meet mine, I see her. She's breaking inside.

With a far-off stare, Oubliette croaks out, "Do you know what my name means?" Not waiting for an answer, she continues as if I said yes. "It's a dark place you toss prisoners. It's a dungeon. It has only one way in and one way out. A trap without end."

Oubliette is an aptly named woman. She doesn't understand that she's my dungeon, my prison, and heartless home in the near future.

Hearing a knock at the outer door of the building, I know that their ride has arrived. Placing an arm under her legs and one around her back, I lay her against my chest and rise. Having her this close is deadly, but necessary. Having her this way will also deter Jasmine from trying to harm me.

Pulling out the fob and punching in the current code, I slide the lock. Opening up the door to the light of day, the sun outside is shocking.

Christ, I've been doing this all night.

"Fuckin' took you long enough," I tell the newcomer.

"Shut your trap, fuckstick. That last group was taken to the airport, headed for Mexico. Don't blast me for the late transport arrangements, brother." Cameron is a guy I grew up in the program with. He's dark as fucking night, smart-mouthed, and a real prince when he's not doing this job. But like me, this asshole's attitude is a necessity.

"Where's the ride?"

With a wave of his hand, he whispers, "Around the corner like before. The cameras can catch our movements better there, leaving evidence."

I can't be implicated. That's imperative.

Now that I have everything ready, the final piece of the board must be placed. I'm the pawn in this game, and I'm hoping that Jazzy's aim will be compromised with her hands cuffed together. Otherwise, I'm dead.

As Cameron removes Jasmine from her cage, we lead them around the corner outside. Opening the back of the SUV and laying Oubli-ette on the seat, I wrap the seatbelt around her. Brushing stray hairs from her face, I want to say more about what we're doing, but I don't. I can't without giving it away.

Stepping back, she doesn't notice she's free, or that she's in a plush vehicle. She doesn't notice anything. I'm hoping that she'll get through this. That the strong woman who told me off, who pushed for answers and that wouldn't turn on the Horsemen, will survive this setback in her life. I tell myself that little lie as I shut the door.

Turning, I find Cameron and Jazzy yelling profanities at one another. "Sly, you done shouting at the woman?"

He laughs. "She's a spitfire. I like her. Can I keep her?"

"No, you dolt. She's his. We have to give her over." I mean her brother, but I need Jasmine unsure of her new home.

The smile disappears, but he still appears interested. "Maybe he won't mind sharing her just a bit then. I mean, he'll have her forever. A few moments aren't important."

I know he doesn't mean it. It's that she needs a reminder she's not in charge. She needs to feel that we're giving her away to some sick fuck.

"Let's go," I say.

"I'm going to enjoy watching you die, Busta. Death comes swiftly, remember?" Jasmine smirks as she quotes her club motto.

"I look forward to it." Pulling her hands close, I start for the back seat of the second SUV. Cameron and I have orchestrated this, so he knows where to stand, where to go, and how to show stupidity. Holding her hands within mine, I click the door open. "Time to go to your new home, bitch." Shoving her forward, she fights me. Kicking wildly, swinging her arms and reaching to grip anything that will assist in her freedom, she plays the part I so desperately need her to play perfectly.

I act sloppy.

I allow her to connect with a few well-timed hits.

I act as if she has the upper hand.

Turning as she aims for my cock, I step sideways and release her hands. I was hoping she'd reach for the gun at my back, and she doesn't disappoint. Aiming for my chest without hesitation, she clips off a round, then points it at Sly. Sly turns slightly, taking a hit to the arm. With him taking a run at her for the gun, it clicks over and over, but nothing happens. That's because there were only two bullets. Only two possible shots, and now she's out of ammo.

Swinging to hit Cameron with everything she's got, I watch and act as if her chest shot was a crippling blow. Falling to the ground and playing the part, Sly wrestles with her for the gun. Eventually she wins, as he fakes that she's knocked him out. She takes the keys to the cuffs and the key to the SUV, while the two of us lie on the ground, acting like we're damaged and unable to fight.

Watching as she takes off out of the lot, as if the wings of hell's carriage are attached to that four-cylinder Ford, she rounds the corner, and then she's out of sight.

We both get to our feet. "Think she bought it?" I ask him.

"More than."

I motion to the cameras around the corner that were filming the charade. "Think they got it too?"

"Absolutely."

CHAPTER 29

Oubliette

As tires squeal and we round corners, I'm still in a daze, but I get it. We're free from that den of hell.

"I don't get it, though, O," Jazzy chirps joyously. "After all the security and the containment, how is it that we were able to get away so easily? I mean, I'm not knockin' it, but shit. We shoulda had more trouble getting away. I'm not *that* good."

Rounding another corner, the speed sends me into the corner of the car door. "I'm not quite sure where we are, but I'll find us a phone to use. Once Death hears of this, he'll rain down fucking hell on their heads. Fucking Broken Bows will be burnt. They'll be the remnant charcoals from a fire I'll light. They'll be laid out on the ground for the wind to bluster." Laughing maniacally, Jasmine is exuberant. I revel in her happiness, even though I'm still dazed by the circumstances.

"Oubliette, I'm so excited to plan their deaths. I truly hope they understand how badly I want their balls in tortillas. *Criadillas* and *Sirrachia*. Mmm. It sounds so yummy."

Turning corners at breakneck speeds, it hurts my neck to swing back and forth, but listening to her voice helps. Her insanity is soothing.

Turning in the seat slightly to look at me, I try a smile. I know it's weak, but at least it's better than sobbing into my soaked, puke-stained shirt, or lying in that cage any longer. Did I think it would break me? That those days in there could do as much damage as they did?

How long had others been in there? How were they able to stay sane? To me, it's a mystery. And now? Now where are they? Those saddened souls have been transported to men and women that will treat them worse than their discarded recycling. I honestly think where they've gone is a fate far worse than death.

Slowing down and stopping the SUV in an alley, Jazzy turns to me, touching my knee. "We'll be home soon, I swear. I swear to you, O, they'll pay for what they've done." Checking the compartments, I watch as she searches for something.

"Ah-ha! Got it." Lifting a gun out of the center armrest and a phone, Jazzy worries more about the phone than the gun. As it lights up, she grins. "Thank fuck it's not locked."

Scrolling through it, she focuses on the GPS. "We're close to the compound. Fuck. With all that moving around, I thought we were in San Fran or something."

I shift on the seat, trying to upright myself. I don't feel any better than I did earlier, at least not mentally, but I'm trying to regain my inner strong girl. I don't like this lack of control. I hated the power they held.

But…Busta? He didn't seem…evil or malicious? He gave me the room, he allowed me to sleep. He stuffed me in the cell, but I saw the look on his face. He didn't want to do it. He felt bad. Jazzy stated that he'd watched me all night, worried for me. That doesn't make sense to me. Why?

It doesn't matter. I'm free, and that's all that matters.

Jazz makes a call. "Hey, Bennett…Slow down. Hold on…I… Just…Wait! I can't tell you if you don't shut up, now can I?" Yelling into the phone, giving her brother shit, I can imagine the attitude he's spewing. He and his sister are as thick as thieves. Jazzy missing must have made him batshit crazy with worry. "No, I get it. Lockdown. Sure…Yeah, I know where we are. We'll go straight there. Yeah…No, I mean it. Of course. Love you too, B."

Hanging up the line, Jazzy taps my knee. Instinctively, I flinch at the contact. "Sorry," she says. I want to reply, but with this throat and how I'm feeling in my head, I can't answer her in a coherent way.

She turns back to the wheel and starts the SUV back up, then tears off out of the alley and back onto the streets.

"I promise, O. They'll know what hell is."

CHAPTER 30

Busta

I'm back at church in San Bernardino. Shit's totally different, but what did I expect? True's in the top seat now. No vote to bring him in, it just is.

My chest hurts like a son of a bitch. The sting aches from the impact on my vest. I'm thankful that True thought to add Kevlar to our cuts a few years back. My life was saved by that thin sheet of material. If DG'd worn one, he would still be alive. Yeah, the cancer would've taken him soon anyway, but the appointment in hell would've been delayed. Now he's six feet under after a bad ride that ended in bullets and blood.

"Everything's fucked up!" True yells, smacking his heavy hand on the table. "Busta takes a bullet, half the cargo went to the wrong clients, and the other half didn't arrive. How the fuck did that happen! Someone better fuckin' have an answer that makes sense to me." I went with the roster that Munch sent over, with a slight variation on two women and a few dead. Church started an hour ago, and it's been a shouting match ever since. Some blame me.

Some blame the transport company. Others figure we were hacked. I've worked that angle to stay out of the limelight.

I'd ridden back to San B in a truck laden with the body of Nock. He was stinky as fuck, but at least the drive wasn't long. He didn't deserve to be left in the empty warehouse, and Nock shoulda been on his Harley. That would've been more appropriate. Going with his pants down would've been a close second in his dreams.

Stomping around, pacing in front of the table, True's sanity is hanging by a thread. "We need this settled fast. Who's going after the Bastards? Who's hitting the Horsemen? We need to hit them hard before they know we're coming. They've already gone into club lockdown, but they're stupid. They've left their businesses vulnerable." Pointing to Flight, Blaze, Miss, and myself, we nod, knowing he's giving us directives. This isn't a democracy, this is a dictatorship. Yeah, DG was that way, and we've been working on adjusting True to work with us as a club, but it's a race, not a sprint, to the finish. Today isn't the day to fight this battle.

"Where do you want us first?" I ask.

"I'm gonna hit the shop over on Second. It's run by Curse's family. He'll feel it," True sneers.

"Family? You wanna go after his family?" Miss questions. We don't hit family, it's an unwritten rule. Holding Death's sister was a direct hit.

He's changed the rules.

"This is our family! No one else matters. If you have an issue with it, the fucking door is there, Miss." Tossing a framed picture of himself and his blood relatives, it smashes off the wall behind Miss.

We're all giving him a wide berth today because of DG's death. We can't fault him for being vindictive or retaliatory. He's working from emotion. As True takes a moment, then visibly calms, he continues with a sick grin. We're all silent as we wait. "This needs to happen quickly, no delays. They need to bleed."

Looking at the rest of the room, taking in the change in leadership, or lack of, True turns to me. "Busta and Miss, you've been promoted." Tossing patches at us, I thumb the VP marker.

I'm kinda shocked, but I don't flinch. Instead, I relax into the wall I'm leaning on. With the fiasco at the warehouse, you'd think he'd take me out back and lay a few shots to my head with his fists, but like I said before, he's going off his own playbook. Changing the guard

and the rules is just another part of that dictatorship.

"Busta, you're VP now. It was always
Strike's, but he's made it quite apparent that he
wants nothing to do with us." He turns to Miss.
"Enforcer is yours. Don't fuck it up."

With a wicked grin, clapping his hands together, he replies greedily, "I won't let you
down, Pres."

"Good. Now, let's get these fuckers. Church
is out, boys. The arrow strikes true."

As we recite it back, one by one, each of us
rise, setting off on our paths, ready to to fuck up
the surrounding clubs. Not everyone believed in
DG's leadership, but that doesn't matter. He
deserves retribution.

Walking into the common room, the boys
are gathering around the bar. Miss and the others are having a celebratory drink before heading out. The room that seemed so sullen and
depressing about a death in the family earlier, is
now ready to take on the death of others.
Though not until there's a drink or two within to
warm the soul.

"One for the road." Quiver states as he
hands out shots across the bar. He's smiling.
It's not a true one, but one for show. I feel for
him. He has to be worrying about his dad. Vic-

tory is an okay guy, and he's trustworthy, just like his sons. I hope he pulls through.

Waving it off, I growl, "Nah, I'm good. I have things to do."

"Suit yourself. Have fun hunting, VP," he says, giving me that knowing grin of his as I start for the door.

Stepping out into the light of day, I head to my bike. Starting her up, enjoying the rumble that I need to forget what's gone on, I start toward the street. Passing the gates and turning left, I see the strangest sight. Something I never thought I'd see in my lifetime.

Strike is walking up to the club gates. In the five years I've been here, Strike's only ever been here intentionally for family functions.

Someone's in for a shock.

Shit's going down, and this won't be good. I can feel it.

Not my circus, though.

I have bigger issues. I have a meeting I'd rather not go to, but one that's necessary because of her, because of the deal I made to save her. One that can break me.

I'm off to see King.

CHAPTER 31

<u>Oubliette</u>

"How are you this morning?" the club doctor, Susan, asks me as she sits on a stool. She's sweet and gentle, and she's impressed me. With doctor ordered doses of drinking this crazy concoction of sugar, honey, and cooled mint tea, I can almost speak a whole sentence without coughing.

"I'm better."

"Let's remove the poultice and see how those bruises are doing then."

Sitting in the common room, I feel like I'm naked with my legs open for an annual. Everyone stares as the bandages are removed—they have for five days straight—as the catty women spew out their snarky remarks. I'm the attention getter. I'm the chick that fought off and 'supposedly' killed a biker from the Bows.

'I hear they're tough as nails.'

'There's no way she did it.'

I'm the bullshitter. It must have been a bad break-up with a boyfriend, or sex that got too rough. I've ignored their constant barbs, but sitting here in the common area with everything on display, it kinda calls for it.

I put my hand on Susan's. "Can we go to another room for this?" Looking over her shoulder, I indicate the audience with my eyes.

Standing up, she grabs her supplies and the stool. "Yeah." She smiles sweetly. "Of course. Lead the way."

We arrived back to a locked-down club where the gates were closed, as well as the club's bars. Humble was shut for 'renovations' and every member they could think of was pulled in for security reasons, me included. Actually, I wasn't given a choice. It was "Get your ass inside and deal with the pampering you'll receive." Jazzy's orders.

Death, from that moment on, insisted that I call him Bennett. He felt totally responsible for the fiasco over Crystal, our captivity, and my near-death experience. So, of course, his sister has pulled out all the stops on payback. My bank account was decidedly fuller when I looked at it yesterday—five figures heavier. I told him to take it back, but he said there was a raise for everyone at Humble.

Liar.

The shit thing about it all, was that the rest of the guys still can't look me in the eyes. They treat me like a victim, or a deity. I'm not sure which yet. Treating me like a victim is something I *despise*. Love me or hate me, but don't pity me. I don't accept pity. Not when my parents died, and definitely not now. I'm stronger than people expect.

I'm the hero in my own story, as well as the suspect. After all, I killed a man.

I'm still not dealing with that very well. It'll take me a long time to get over seeing those eyes. The look as he realized his death was near. I think of it every time I close my own eyes, every time I'm alone, and when I'm reminded of how strong I was.

I'm not as strong as I think—not near enough. I'm acting a part. It's been a deadly dance, one that I can't deal with knowing the outcome.

Opening the door to my borrowed room, Susan follows me.

"Have a seat on the bed, sweetie," she states.

Having a seat on the stool she carried down the hall with her, I sit on the edge of the bed and raise my head slightly. Smiling weakly, I lift my chin.

Pulling at the tape, releasing the edge of the bandage, Susan unravels it. Careful to avoid my hair, I hold my ponytail up. It takes a minute, but once she has the gauze off and the poultice removed, she smiles.

"Wow. This is looking terrific." She begins working on a new one. "I was worried. I thought with the pressure marks you had, there would be permanent scars."

Picking up the borrowed compact that Jazzy gave me, I look. When I first arrived here, sullen, self-contained, and internally imploding, I wouldn't look in the mirror. I couldn't bring myself to see the monster inside. I know it's only been five days, but it's a lifetime that I stole from Nock.

Shaking off the darkness and danger of falling down that rabbit hole again, I smile as I look at myself. "It looks totally better."

"Well, I think we need a few more days with this so that lovely skin of yours doesn't end up with any permanent scarring."

"I think I deserve a permanent scar," I mutter.

Taken aback by my response, I see the disappointment on Susan's face as clearly as if it were typed out. "Don't do that to yourself. You did what you had to do to survive. I heard all about it from Jazzy. You didn't have a choice, between him breaking your body and your mind. You can't think that way. You did what you had to do."

"Yeah, I guess so."

She playfully smacks my leg. "Know so." Susan means it in fun, but still, I flinch.

"Sorry," I say.

Leaning forward with the poultice, she wraps it around the sides. "Nothing to say sorry for. Remember that, Oubliette."

Remember. That's all I'm doing.

For the next twenty minutes I sit, allowing Susan to wrap my sore throat.

As she readies herself to leave, Destroyer barges through the door. Turning to me, his look switches away quickly. Again, that pity or deity gaze. I really wish I knew which one it was. At least I could get over it. We used to have a good understanding at Humble. I gave the drinks out, and I knew more of their troubles than most. I thought we were…friends.

"Doc, we need you. Curse was hit." Squinting his eyes at me and turning heel down the hall, he's gone faster than I can blink.

The disappointment must be written on my face, as Susan responds with, "It'll be okay. They'll come around." She walks to the door with her supplies. "I'll check on you tomorrow."

Wincing, I attempt a true smile. I try to show my best brave face.

"I'll be fine. Swear."

Walking out of the room, I head back to the common area, where there's a flurry of activity. Curse is laid out on the pool table, with Susan tending to a chest wound. This is when I feel useless. This is when I feel out of place. This is when I'm reminded that I don't belong here.

"Someone grab me some whiskey!" Susan shouts. The old man who I've come to adore— the growly, surly Thanos, isn't behind the bar. He's standing at the pool table, holding the hand of his son, Curse. As he screams and squirms from the pain, I start for the bar. Grabbing booze is something I can do.

Stepping behind the bar, pulling up the half-finished bottle of whiskey, I take it to Susan's waiting hand. "Here. Anything else?"

Taking the bottle, she answers me while tending to Curse's wound. "Thanks, Oubliette. Thanos, we need to get him to the hospital."

"Where the fuck is he!" Blowing the door wide open and rushing to the table, Death is by Curse's side in seconds, his face a mix of emotions. "Had to do it all alone. I told you, I said...I said not to, didn't I? Why won't you learn, Wally?"

"I…couldn't stop them. I'm…sorry."

"Who was it? Who did this?" I've seen Death fun, I've seen him serious, but this is a sight I'm glad I've never seen. He's ready to kill.

He tries to speak, but winces through the pain, causing his answer to come out unintelligible.

"Who? Who was it, Curse?" Death pressurizes his teeth, his body vibrating from the anger that courses through him.

"Bows," he answers, as his eyes roll back and he passes out.

"Death, we have to move him. He needs a hospital." Susan's holding bandages to the wound, trying to stop the flow. They're dark, stained from the blood coating them. If they wait any longer, Curse won't live to tell who it was exactly.

"I have the van up front. Thanos, you and Doc will go in the back, yeah?" Death turns to his sister. "Jazzy, keep things locked down."

"Got it."

Another person dying because of me— because I saw Bracken kill his sister. Another that I can't help.

Holding back the bile, my eyes are trained on the death that surrounds me.

Despair is beginning to sit heavy on my soul.

CHAPTER 33

Oubliette

The clubhouse got crazy nuts. Returning from the bathroom, where I wretched out the remainder of what I'd eaten—which was pretty much nothing—I stood idly by as the room became a flurry of activity. Guys ran around grabbing up weapons, emptying the common room, shuttling wives, girlfriends, and kids to their bedrooms.

Susan, Thanos, Death, and a compliment of riders left for the hospital, leaving a blood-soaked pool table and four dead bodies strewn across the room on the floor. Curse's sister, her husband, and two other members I'd only seen a handful of times in Humble, all dead. Staring at the disaster around me, seeing Nock's dead eyes as he laid in a pool of his own blood, takes me back to that cage. That hell.

Feeling bile rise in my throat again, I race from the room, pushing my way by. Hitting the bathroom of my borrowed bedroom, I wretch into the toilet. The reminders of that place hit me like a wall every time I turn. Sleeping or awake, Nock's eyes shock me. Blood is a reminder of a death I created. Not even puking can help me release the fear and pain I feel at being that person.

"Oubliette?" Poking her head in my room as the guys ran off to deal with Curse, Jazzy was super frightened. Something had her spooked.

"Hey. How we doing?" she asks me with a fake grin.

"What's going on, Jaz?"

"Nothing—"

"Liar. Don't lie to me. I can handle—"

She raises her hand, cutting me off. "No, you can't." Stepping further into the room and closing my door, Jazzy pushes up against it. "Babe, shit's going down and it's best we hide out."

Crossing my legs and sitting on the bed, I pat it in mocking fun. "What, like watch movies, braid each other's hair and talk about boys? Come on. Tell me what's going on."

She's seemingly frustrated, but I know she'll give in if I bug her a bit more.

I don't wait long. "It's best you stay here, Oubliette. I know you've worked at Humble, but that's so different from being in a clubhouse on lockdown. It's not safe out there right now." Shifting away from it, popping the door open and starting for the hall, she says over her shoulder, "Please, stay here," she pleads. "Please."

"Tell me what's going on and I will. Fair?"

"I can't. You're here for protection, but you're not a part of this."

"I don't think I'm a part of it, but I'm not on the outside of it anymore either." Pointing to my neck, I remind her that I've seen things I'd rather not acknowledge, even in my worst nightmares.

"Please stay here. Just keep out of the way," she says curtly.

As I nod and smile, I answer, "Okay, Jazzy. I'll stay away from there. Promise." I lie.

"Thanks, O. I'll feel better knowing you're safe."

What a relative term.

Walking out, closing the door behind her, I'm left alone to my own demons. This isn't a friendly place for me. I feel awful alone, but even worse when I see reminders of it everywhere I turn. Nothing here is mine, everything is borrowed. The death and destruction is an attachment of this lifestyle I've been thrust into.

I need to go home.

It's not like I'm of any use here anyway, or needed. What am I going to do, pour drinks?

I pull on a pair of trainers. Checking the hall, seeing the exit at the side is clear, I start toward it. Everyone must be in their rooms already, or helping in the common area. Maybe I can get out undetected.

As I hit the edge of the building and turn to the street entrance, I look at the front gate. Guys are funneling out on Harley's, one after the other, and heading south. Once the last has left, Malice, and Jazzy's little brother, Apoc, close up the gates.

Each step I take is with determination. This isn't where I belong. My condo won't afford me guns and scary bikers, but I need my bed, my large tub, my coffee, my whiskey, and my space. I need to be where I belong.

"Where do you think you're going?" Malice asks as I move close.

"I'm going home. Death said I was okay to go. There's no use in me staying here any longer." I'm just a burden, I think to myself. "I'm going home. You have bigger issues than me."

Knowing I've told the truth, that I really am a burden, and that they have bigger problems, it's easy to talk them into it.

"If you have any problems, I can't guarantee that we can help you. You sure?" Apoc asks. He's a sweet kid. Not patched in yet, he's the perfect younger replica of his brother.

Smiling sweetly, I say, "Yeah, I'm good."

Pushing the gate part way, Apoc let's me leave. It isn't without an argument from Malice, but I make them see my side.

CHAPTER 34

Busta

I remember the day I walked out of the Cruel Intentions clubhouse. It all hangs in my memory like a dream…or a nightmare.

The dark, wood grain paneling, a stark contrast against the light gray walls that housed old pictures of members gone, motorcycles that had seen better days from wrecks, and the odd shadow boxes with a piston, or chunk of leather captioned with 'Joe's first Harley' or 'In Memory of…'

That was the club I knew, loved, and left when I *had* to. I did it to keep those I loved safe. So it's funny that the club I walked into as a DEA agent is *now* my family. I'm a Bow. I'm a Bow through and through. I never patched into my step-father's club, but I always felt that their 1% was cleaner and better than what I'm involved in now.

It was all a lie. I know the Bows are no cleaner than the Intentions were. I figured that out quickly.

I was seventeen when the DEA raided our club. I hadn't patched yet, and I was so pissed that they'd pulled me in to be their snitch. I didn't have a choice then, not really. It was either go to jail as a snitch, because that's what they were going to label me as, or watch my family get destroyed. My little brother and sister deserved a chance to grow up with our parents, instead of children's aid and foster care, so I did what I felt was best at the time.

To the DEA, I was the perfect weapon. I knew the life, I loved being in it, and I was angry at them for what they did to us. For the next five years, they trained me, taught me what they expected out of me, and left me with enough guilt that if I didn't do it right, I couldn't save those I cared for. When I graduated their 'program', the DEA sent me off with only one contact, King. The man has the attitude of a dangerously starved bear, and is the size of Dwayne Johnson. I'm not fearful of going toe-to-toe with him anymore, but I doubt that we'd have a clear winner.

Magnus King is an asshole. He's *the* asshole.

I guess we both are, 'cause yeah, they may have dragged me kicking and screaming, but I've knowingly kept myself in the game as their tool. I knew that one day I might need their leverage, but I should've tossed his DEA tag back at him when I'd patched into the Bows five years ago. I didn't. When I knew what they do/did/are, I should've closed off that portion of my life.

So today, here I am, pulling into a meet with King. It was a part of the deal I struck, as he helped clear out the warehouse. I hate it, but it was necessary.

Making sure I wasn't followed, I head into the south end of San B after an indirect route and pull into the parking garage. No one knows I'm here. I don't even want to be here, but I am for one reason and one reason only.

Her.

Obi.

Seeing her distraught, seeing her torturing herself over a death she couldn't avoid, it crushed me. I couldn't leave her to that fate. Reminded of why I'm doing this, my mind wanders to that day at Humble, the days at the warehouse, and every waking moment since.

I can't get that woman out of my head. She's dug her claws in deep, and I'm stuck in her clutches. She did nothing to cause this, other than being a strong woman that defied what I thought couldn't. I expected a weak-minded, soft shell that couldn't hold her own. She surpassed that. She was broken, but she didn't break.

Making it through the doors, the enclosed area compresses the noise of my bike as I roll in. I love the throaty sound of my custom as it moves through, the sound bouncing back in a symphony of Harley Davidson exhaust.

Level after level, the parking garage is stoically empty of cars, trucks, and motorcycles. Hell, even people. As my eyes adjust, I see the outline of King near the backlit elevator bank, arms and ankles crossed, waiting impatiently for me. Pulling up beside him, I park and shut off my ride.

I'm not giving him power.

I take my time because I know it'll piss him off. I called in one favor in a long line of owed favors. The last time I saw him, I was young and afraid to cause strife, but now I don't give a fuck. I'm not a pushover anymore. I'm not some cunt kid he can kick around.

"You don't call. You don't write. Then, out of nowhere, with high fucking expectations that we save—"

"Don't bullshit me, King. You've been waiting for my call." Crossing my arms, I stare at him. I won't allow him the upper hand. I'm a bigger asshole than he is now, and even if I do have ties to him and his DEA, I'm a scary motherfucker who takes no shit.

Staying quiet for a moment, King looks me up and down, sizing up his chances. I'd say we're evenly matched. Son of a bitch will be hurting when I'm done. In all honesty, he deserves a few good shots to the head, and I might do it for fun.

"New position, eh?" he asks, surprising me.

Again, I stay quiet.

Pushing off the wall, he starts toward me with a knowing grin. The sick bastard has something in mind. "I think VP will suit you fine for the short-term, *Busta.* Pres might be better."

With confusion and suspicion, I growl out, "What the fuck are you talking about?"

"There's always room at the top for the right man, don't you think?"

Rising off the bike swiftly and stomping his way, I shove King against the wall. I don't hear anything but his bones rattling. "What the fuck are you talking about?"

Laughing haughtily, a smug smile crosses his face. "Let's just say we have a need for a man at the gavel. Someone we can trust. We want to do business with the Bows and I need you fully integrated."

Pressing my forearm into his throat, causing him to push his neck back, he laughs even harder.

Sick fuck.

Sticking a gun to my side, I hear the click. "You may not be a punk kid anymore, Lucius, but you still don't think of the bigger picture. You're not VP material. The Bows need a new president. They need a new mandate. They *need* you."

"Who's your snitch? If it isn't me, who told you about the new appointment? It was only announced an hour ago." I look down at my cut. "I don't even wear the patch yet."

"Best you don't put that VP on there. It's a lot of work to do it twice."

Pushing off of him, a little of my fire dies down. I want information more than I want to kill him. "What's your angle?"

"My angle has always been the same. I need someone in the ranks that can help us close the corruption gap in the West Coast MC's."

"And if I deny you—"

"Your sister is doing great in her new city. And your brother, he's done exceptionally well. I'd hate to see things change."

Punching him in the face, the bones vibrate. It feels good to hurt him. It feels good to do damage after the week I've had.

Spitting out a mouthful of blood, King smirks. "You've grown up, kid. This life suits you. Just remember that jail won't help those you love."

Hitting him again and again, he smiles as I land every punch. With a quick, sharp left, King hits me hard in the stomach. It's not enough to wind me, but it's enough to give me pause.

Taking a step back, I reach for my gun and aim it at his head, just as he's now doing to me. His dark grin kicks up a notch. "You don't want to do that, and I don't want to lose you. So let's say we agree to disagree, Lucius."

Before I can ask him further questions, or take the definitive shot at his head, my phone rings. King's smile is perfectly evil and smug.

"Great timing. Better take that."

Scowling, I look at the number. Not dropping my guard or lowering my gun, I look at the screen. It's Miss.

"Yeah, go."

"Brother, shit's gone down. We need you now."

To be continued in Pawn.

FROM THE AUTHOR,

Sorry.

Okay, so maybe I'm not sorry, but I couldn't give you the whole story in one shot. Here's why.

If you haven't picked up the anthology, The 7, you missed the story that started it all. Envy was my contribution to the anthology, and your introduction to the Broken Bows. If you've read The 7, Envy, then you know where this story goes for the Madox brothers. If not, I was giving it away in the rest of Oubliette's and Busta's story if I didn't take a short commercial break. So, instead of a lovely little 'Hi, how are ya' at the beginning of the book, I decided to write you a note at the end.

To thank you during your wait, The 7, Envy, is available through this link free, exclusively on Instafreebie. Read it so that you're up to speed on the destruction that has occurred in their lives.

If you've read it, and are now wanting to skin me alive for stopping short, don't worry…

Book Two, Pawn will release August 2018.

I can't give you a teaser into the next book, as it gives away Envy's storyline. So instead, here's a snippet of another story to keep you interested in my dark and twisted mind until the release in a short few weeks.

Love as always,

The sick, twisted bitch,
KERRI ANN

#evilauthorkerriann
#brokenbowsmc

Excerpt from:

ROOK

The Broken Bows Book 1.5

BY

KERRI ANN

Chapter One

"Forgive me, Father, for I have sinned,"
the small voice from the other side of the screen
confided. I can just make out her shadow as
she completes the sign of the cross. "Today
marks the fifteenth day since my last confession. My last mass was three weeks ago, and I
have one sin to atone for."

"Tell me your troubles, child." I know it's
fruitless to ask, but it's expected. Their whole
reason for appearing here is to be absolved.

"I had impure thoughts about a woman in
my...book club," she says cautiously.

"Are you lying, child?"

"Father, I'm telling you what I feel comfortable with you knowing." So, she's another one of *them*.

 "Continue, child."

She clears her throat. "You see, we were reading a book about first loves. It was about a woman, and how her best friend was the first to really *see* her through all her faults. Her problems didn't matter. Seeing love conquer and repair damages, she came to love the other woman—in the story, that is. Love can be pure in so many ways. Right, Father?"

"Yes, child. I agree that love can be pure of heart, but not sexual in its context, such as love thy brother, love thy sister. What is it, though, that has made you feel impure? Tell me. Tell your God what it is so that you may repent." Every day, all day, this is the possible outcome of so many lives in our city. These lost souls need our care, and it's my job to make them whole. They need to feel loved and cherished without reservation or condemnation.

"Well, Father, I've never felt that from a man. It made me feel secure and cared for by this woman. She makes me feel like I'm perfect. I *know* in my heart that God would tell me if this love is wrong. But if love is good in all forms, then why deny me a love if he presents it?"

And there's the predicament of my position. How can I deny love? How do I tell her that it's an abomination to love another woman in the way that she does? I do the will of God because it's right and just. "What you personally feel is different than the scriptures, my dear child. Loving in a chaste way is expected and condoned, but to love her in the way that a man and a woman would is unwell in the eyes of God."

"But Father, what of the changes under the Pope, the holiest of Fathers on earth? Hasn't he stated that all love is to be cherished? Why deny me? My confession isn't in loving *her*, my confession is this; In loving her, the love for my husband has become secondary. I love him, I do, but I can't love him as I love her. Do you understand, Father?"

So, it's not that she loves this woman, it's that she's venturing out of her marriage. Well, this one's cut and dry. "This is an impure allowance under God and his teachings. You must care for your wedding vows. You will work on giving your husband the love and devotion that you imparted when you first married him. You gave your word that his love was the only love, other than that of your God."

"Yes, Father." Her voice falls. Seeing her bowing her head in defeat, I wonder...did she really feel that her confession would be seen as a just reason to venture from wedlock and step out of the marriage? These are the situations I deal with, and it pains me. Our parish is in a more volatile area of the city, which brings these creatures of faithlessness to our door often.

"You will repent your sins through your act of contrition. Repeat after me, 'Heavenly Father, I in good faith will follow the path of your teachings, and in doing so, I will work on being a good person that puts effort into my marriage.'" She quietly repeats what I say, and I continue. "I will no longer have impure thoughts about another, as it is unfair to my vows under God." She again repeats after me, and in doing so, I hear her voice becoming stronger; more willful.

"You will perform six hail Mary's and continue to work on your family obligation. I absolve you of your sins. In the name of the Father, and of the Son, and of the Holy Spirit. Amen."

"Amen. Thank you, Father." Rising out of the booth, she closes the door behind her while I relax with another completed parishioner on the right path. Do I analyze every one of these sad souls? Yes. I care for them, not only as their direct link to Christ, but I also feel their pain and sorrow as their priest.

There are days that these burdens weigh heavily on my soul, and that I despair with the inflicted damage on my own psyche. My lord keeps me strong, or as strong as he can. And what I cannot handle, I contain in my own way.

Her love of the woman could be a product of a bad relationship. The dangerous liaison could be nothing more than her looking for love where love hasn't been found yet. Nervously rubbing the sleeve of my robes, I take a deep breath and blow it out. I'll deal with the dark thoughts I have about her and the love she has later when I'm alone.

As the door next to me opens and closes again, a man enters. "Forgive me, Father, for I have sinned."

Garnering my composure to assist another lost soul once more, I situate myself in the confessional to take on their needs. "Tell me how I can help you, son."

"It's been six months since my last confession." His voice is deep and gruff. His voice has a dangerous tone that's truly recognizable—hardened and callous.

Answering him in a calm manner, I say, "Six months is a long time. How many confessions will we address today?"

The screen doesn't allow room for me to see his face, but I can see his profile. I know who he is. Bracken Madox, President of the Broken Bows MC. His club runs the south side of the city with an iron will, and even heavier fist. They deal in guns, drugs, and sex trading. He's a dangerous man.

"Only those I wish you to know, Father." Bracken and I have history, and I both love and loathe when he visits.

"To absolve you, I would expect nothing more than full honesty, my son."

He laughs darkly. "How about I give you what I can, Father. The rest is for you to read between the lines. I think my wife is stepping out. Mostly my fault. I think I push her to it."

Great. The woman that was here is his wife. Just the darkness I needed today. Thank you, Father, for giving me a further trial of piety.

"Knowing if she has stepped out is not yours to confess. Tell me your confession, son."

"You're right, Father." His sinister voice booms off the walls of our tiny enclosure. "My sins are extensive. How long do you have?"

I don't doubt they are. Lifting the edge of my cassock, I scratch the scars on my wrist. "As long as you need, son."

"Well, let's get started then, shall we?" Laying his long legs out in front of him, Bracken crosses his ankles, settling in for a long conversation. "My first sin, of course, has multiple in-

fractions. Sins of the flesh. I love flesh. I've partaken in free pussy that would make your robes
curl, Father. The taste of that sweet nectar as it
glides along your tongue? Mmm, exquisite. The
feel of supple tits as they're pinched, fucked,
scarred and sucked? The heavy screams as
they ask to be released? Yeah, that's both dangerous and intoxicating. But you wouldn't understand that, would you, *Kyden*? No. You
wouldn't know the feel of a woman's cunt anymore. You walked away from that."

Walking isn't the right, I ran. Slipping
away in the middle of the night, I left, never
looking back. He knows that every time he explains his sins, the effect is meant to shock. He
understands it more than any other could. He
knows me. A woman's touch is not what I need,
though I'd love it. The reminder is fresh every
moment. Clearing my throat, I try to bring the
conversation back to something more suitable
for the venue. "Thank you for the honesty, son.
You stated multiple sins—"

"Yes, that I did. I've been having difficul-
ties expressing my rage. It comes out in fits of
destructiveness." His tone is excited. I can almost see his snarky grin.

"You have released this rage on others, I
assume?" Catching my nail on one of the more
recent scars, I revel at the pain it elicits.

"Goddamn right I have."

"We do not take the Father's name in vain here, son. Please refrain from blaspheme, or I'll have to ask you to leave without completing your penance."

"Yes, Priest. I understand the consequences." Uncrossing his ankles and shifting forward on the seat, Bracken brings his face close to the screen. "I understand perfectly."

"Good. Continue, please."

"Well, Father, I've unfortunately harmed a few poor souls in my care."

"Harming others is not permitted. Do unto others as you wish done upon you. Follow the path of God's will and you will find absolution."

"I think I'm past the point of absolution. Don't you, Ky?"

"My name is Father Kyden. Please, use it correctly, son."

"Yes, Father Kyden. Thank you for the reminder." His voluminous voice surrounds me, pulling me down that dangerous edge. The reason I became a priest was because of men like him. My darkness envelopes me the same way as his harnesses the truly dangerous parts of him by feeding him, fueling his need for mayhem. "Well, you see, there have been casualties left in my wake. A multitude of corpses. Some I killed with my bare hands, others I had decommissioned by the hands of another, but I was the instrument. Can I be absolved of those sins, Father?"

The itch on my skin is a burning need, a harsh fire of release cresting under the surface. Forcing my hands away and laying them in my lap, I do my best to avoid the need to drive out my inner demons.

Knowing Bracken doesn't wish to repent is not a part of the confessional, though I do wish it were. There's no savior that could clear the taint on Bracken's soul. The devil has held him tight to his bosom for far too long. "I will pray for you, son. Beyond that, it is up to you to repent and see to your own eternal soul. God cannot help you if you do not attempt to atone."

"Understood. Thank you." The glee is palpable in his voice. He's enjoying this far too much.

"Is that the extent of your sins?"

Shaking his head, he looks directly at me. "No, Father. No, no, no, no. I have partaken in one of the worst sins that one can. I've tainted one of God's children that felt they were unattainable." Scratching his fingers down the screen, popping over the holes one by one, slowly, he peers through and glares at me. "I've tainted the soul of a priest. I've reminded him of what he's hiding from, what it is that he covets. What he wishes for. What his *darkest* desires are." The darkness of evil is visible in his gaze as he stares through the screen. I feel the inky darkness he talks of, the unwanted caresses that make me shake.

"Who is it that you've tainted, son?"

Sitting back hard against the confessional cabinet, it vibrates under his weight. "You, brother. It may not be today, but it will be soon. You've hidden for long enough. Come home." Rising quickly to his feet, he exits the confessional before I can respond.

ALSO BY KERRI ANN:

MC Series
KING
ROOK
PAWN
QUEEN coming 2019
KNIGHT coming 2019

Crashed Series
BOOK ONE
BOOK TWO
BOOK THREE
BOOK FOUR
BOOK FIVE (TIED) CROSSOVER RUSHED AND
CRASHED M/M STORY

Suspense/Erotica Thriller
LAST BREATH

Suspense/Crime
CHARGED
SPARKED coming 2019

Suspense/Erotica Romance
RUSHED
BOOK FIVE (TIED) CROSSOVER RUSHED AND
CRASHED M/M STORY
RUSHING coming 2019

Paranormal Romance
FATE OF AMBER
FATE OF MINE coming 2019

Anchor Series
MAST coming 2019
KEEL coming 2020
UNTITLED coming 2020

21105621R00129

Made in the USA
Columbia, SC
15 July 2018